PAST FORWARD

ALSO BY JUSTIN RICHARDS

Time Runners 1: Freeze-Framed
Time Runners 2: Rewind Assassin

and in the *Invisible Detective* series:
The Paranormal Puppet Show
Shadow Beast
Ghost Soldiers
Killing Time
The Faces of Evil
Web of Anubis
Stage Fright
Legion of the Dead

TIME RUNNERS

PAST FORWARD

JUSTIN RICHARDS

SIMON AND SCHUSTER

SIMON AND SCHUSTER
First published in Great Britain by Simon and Schuster UK Ltd, 2008
A CBS COMPANY

1 3 5 7 9 10 8 6 4 2

Simon & Schuster UK Ltd
Africa House
64–78 Kingsway
London WC2B 6AH

A CIP catalogue record for this book is
available from the British Library

ISBN: 978-1-41692-644-3

Typeset by Rowland Phototypesetting Ltd,
Bury St Edmunds, Suffolk
Printed and bound in Great Britain by
Cox & Wyman Ltd, Reading Berks

For Tobey – mini-runner!

CHAPTER ONE

It was five years after the president died and time was standing still.

Time had not been kind to America since President Carlton's death. But that wasn't our problem. Anna and I stood outside the orphanage and watched the children being led to the bus. It was an old school bus – yellow and chunky, discoloured, rusty and peppered with bullet holes. There was heavy steel mesh across the inside of the windows. Nope, the United States of America was not a good place to be, not for kids, not for us, not for anyone. Not any more.

The driver had a gun in a holster at his hip. He

1

was frozen, caught in the middle of urging the children on board the bus.

'They don't look frightened,' I said. 'Do they even know what's going on?'

'Do we?' Anna asked. 'Anyway, they're probably used to being moved around.'

'Probably,' I agreed. There was a sadness etched on their faces that was rubbing off on me.

Anna's my friend. One of my only friends now. My best friend. Like me, she's lost. Not lost as in 'can't find her way home'. Lost as in 'fell through one of the cracks in time that people like you can't see'. Now she doesn't exist, and neither do I.

I used to be Jamie Grant. I used to be a twelve-year-old kid who went to school and had a mum and dad and sister and hated history and dreaded PE. But that all changed and now I'm a Time Runner. Anna and I – we get to fix time when it goes wrong. Not that people like you would notice.

We were on a mission now – a 'run' – for our boss, Senex. Sent to sort out some time travel experiments which were much too early and far too successful. So we didn't care that

America was tearing itself apart and falling into violent chaos. We had far more important things to deal with.

And the first thing to deal with was getting on a bus taking eight children from the St Cuthbert's Orphanage in Maryland to ... Well, we'll get to that. First we have to be on the bus. That's why we stopped time and froze everyone in a single split moment.

The strangest thing was the utter silence. Like the air had stopped too – which I suppose it had. No birds, no breeze, no crunch of feet on gravel, no distant gunfire ... The orphanage was fortunate. It had its own grounds and was hidden away behind high fences and barbed wire. They still got some government money, I think. Maybe someone important once went there – someone who still had some clout and could get things done. Or maybe they were just lucky.

There were four boys and four girls. All between about ten and sixteen. All right, the youngest was ten years, three months and nine days old, the oldest sixteen years, eight months, six days. And if you really want to know, seven hours, eleven minutes and seventeen seconds. I could tell. Just by looking at them, I could tell. I can do that – time and I have a sort of understanding. I understand bits of it and in return it ignores me.

'What about these two?' Anna said. She was standing by the last two in the line – a boy and a girl. Both about twelve (I won't bore you with their exact ages).

'Last out,' I said. 'They could have been swapped. It's possible.'

'Anything's possible.' Anna had already decided, and I wasn't going to disagree. She's pretty determined, pretty confident, pretty ... Well, just *pretty*, really. She's got a bob of blonde hair and really green eyes and she looks fourteen – that's how old she was when she was lost. She behaves like she's my older sister. Or something.

'You want to do it?' I asked.

Anna looked away. 'You're better than me at this sort of thing now,' she said. She turned back, looking sort of resigned. I don't think she liked the fact that I was overtaking her in the working-with-time stuff.

'OK,' I said, not wanting to dwell on it.

I reached for the black dial on my wrist. But actually, I didn't need it for something easy like this, not any more. They'd told me – Senex and Anna (and Midnight, but we'll come to him later) – that I've got a talent for working with time. A knack. One day I'll be an Adept. That's like premiership stuff. So I pretended, hoping Anna wouldn't feel so bad if she thought I needed the time dial.

I did what I needed to – even though I don't really know how I do it. It just sort of happens. I guess the footballer doesn't think through each and every muscle or movement when he takes the penalty or slams home a great goal. He just does it. It's like that for me too (only without the football).

The two kids flickered, then faded. We could still see them, but it was like they were a heat haze or a faint painting on glass. Caught between instants of time, in a split second. We'd let them out again, back into real time, once we'd finished our job. And they'd complete the step, the breath, the thought they were in the middle of as if nothing had happened. Though it would be days later.

And the bus would be gone, and we'd have been on it instead of them. Which was good news as far as they were concerned . . . Scary as hell for us.

The driver counted us on. When Anna reached the bus, he put out his hand to stop her.

'Who are you?' he demanded. His voice was a rough, gravelly drawl and his hand was never far from his holster.

'Anna,' she said, meeting his accusing stare. 'Who are you?'

'I'm Jamie,' I said quickly. He was going to ask anyway. 'We got told to come instead of those other two. Just now. By Mrs . . .' My voice tailed off as I realised I'd not really done my homework here. 'You know,' I finished lamely.

'You talk weird,' the driver said, still looking at us suspiciously. Then he stepped aside and nodded towards the bus.

'We're British,' Anna told him as she stepped up into the vehicle. 'It's you that talks weird.'

'Yeah. Right. Funny girl.'

The other kids were all chatting quietly to each other. They got louder and more confident as the bus doors hissed shut and the engine stuttered into life. A couple of them stared at us, then looked quickly away. They came from a world where you didn't ask questions.

Anna and I sat together about halfway back. There were loads of spare seats. No seat belts, and the seat covers were slashed and stained.

'Now listen up,' the driver shouted. He didn't bother to turn round to look at us, just glanced up at his mirror as he started the bus moving. 'This is going to take a while, maybe a coupla hours, and it ain't going to be fun. We'll get there fine, so long as you do what you're told and keep your heads down. And I mean keep your heads down. Whenever I tell you. If I say duck, you duck. If I say get under the seats, you lie down under the seats. You got that?'

There were nods and murmurs and grunts.

'Cos if you don't got that,' he went on with a callous disregard for grammar, 'it's you who's in trouble, big time. Any of you gets shot, it ain't on my conscience. I got my own kids to worry about. Right?'

'Right,' I murmured. Along with about half the other children.

My mate Ben knows loads of song from the

Scouts and gets us singing them on school trips. Or rather, he used to. Before I changed schools, and before I was lost. I didn't think we'd be singing any songs on this trip.

We went for a whole half-hour before anyone shot at us. Maybe they weren't shooting at *us*, but it was close by and bullets dinged off the side of the bus. We were under the seats before the driver yelled. He kept yelling as he put his foot down and the bus roared through the streets.

I heard sirens in among the guns. An explosion. The crackle of fire. Something smacked into the window above me, leaving a spider's web of cracks. I was grateful for the steel mesh.

'What's going on?' I asked Anna. She was lying beside me.

'No-go area,' she said. 'Let's take a look.'

Abruptly the gunfire and the sirens and the driver's yells stopped. Everything stopped and we stood up to take a look at the freeze-framed scene outside. The bus was speeding between two groups of people. There didn't seem to be any way of knowing who was on which side – a mix of clothes, races, men and women on both sides – even children as young as those on the bus. As young as us. All with guns, blazing away at each other. Even though everything had stopped, I could still smell the bitter, smoky gunpowder in the air. I could feel the rush of adrenaline and the fear in the back of my throat all the way down to my stomach.

There was a flash of flame erupting from the end of one gun as it was caught in mid-fire. Across the street, a man was hanging in the air. He looked about twenty at most – being thrown backwards by the force of the bullets that had just hammered into him.

'OK,' I said. 'That's gross.'

'Horrible,' Anna agreed. 'Pointless. Just gang warfare. Everything falling apart.'

'Land of the free,' I muttered. 'How long does this journey take?'

Anna had done her homework, so she knew. 'Another two hours seven minutes, near enough. There's another street fight yet, two more no-go areas. One pitched battle with the police militia forces and a roadblock at the edge of Washington, DC, where a man in the car in front gets shot because he gives the guards some lip.'

9

'Glad I came.'

'You wanted to get a feel for the period,' she reminded me.

I hadn't forgotten.

'And you said we'd be accepted easier if we came in on the bus with the other kids rather than just turning up inside the compound with no excuse,' I said.

'True. We'd better get going, then.'

'Let's hurry it up,' I said. 'We might have to be here, but we don't have to go through it for the whole two hours, seven minutes.'

So we lay on the floor under the seats again and speeded time up. The gunfire became a fast, ripping sound and the sirens were sudden screeches. As we approached the compound, Anna slowed everything down to normal again and we climbed up into our seats, trying to look as if we'd been huddled frightened on the floor. Like everyone else. I don't think anyone noticed anything weird.

Most of the glass had gone from the window and there was a chill breeze coming through the ragged, sharp edges. I brushed slivers of broken glass off the seat before sitting down again, trying not to cut my hands. And failing. I sucked at the heel of my palm where it was bleeding – a sharp, clean pain like a paper cut with the volume turned up.

'Are we nearly there yet?' I joked, looking down the length of the bus and through the crazed windscreen.

'I hope so,' Anna said. She didn't sound like she was joking and I could see why.

The bus had turned into a narrow road. At the far end we could see huge metal gates. But between us and the gates was an angry mob – people with guns, shovels, baseball bats. Lots of them were women and children, but there were some men too. They looked thin and tired, broken into shards and fractured by the maze of cracks on the windscreen. But they had heard and seen the bus and were hurrying towards us with a grim determination.

The most frightening thing was their eyes – blank, staring, dead. I don't mean they were zombies or anything like that. It was only later I realised what was missing and it wasn't actually life as such.

It was hope.

'Hold tight!' the driver shouted. 'We're going through.'

The noise of the engine deepened as he dropped down a gear and the bus juddered with extra power.

Anna clutched my arm. The other children were grabbing each other too – even those still under the seats. The mob outside was shouting and screaming. I couldn't hear any actual words or phrases, but I got the gist of it – through the fug of fear that held me immobile. Too terrified even to reach for my time dial.

They wanted food. They wanted help. They wanted to know what was going on and why the army was there if not to help and protect them.

A woman was spread-eagled across the windscreen, just for a second. Then she was gone, I tried not to think where – thrown aside as the bus surged forwards again. It was shuddering as it tried to push through the mass of bodies pressed up close. Hands slammed against the metal mesh close to Anna and she screamed and held me even tighter. I pulled her clear of clutching fingers.

The barrel of a handgun appeared through the

mesh, aimed right at us. I just stared. Anna froze. We could die. Even though we didn't exist, we could still die, just like anyone else. And it looked as if this might be the time.

The sound of the shot was deafeningly loud.

The gunfire seemed to echo round the inside of the bus. Children flinched and cried out. The gun was pulled quickly back, away from the mesh – the gun that thankfully hadn't fired.

Then the crowd seemed to thin out. More shots – and I realised that, like that first shot, they were all coming from outside the bus. That was what had scared off the guy with the gun pointing at us. As the people cleared away, shouting and protesting and screaming abuse at us, I could see the massive gate in front of us sliding slowly to one side. Standing in front of it was a line of troops – khaki uniforms against the gunmetal grey of the gate, and of the second identical gate fifteen metres behind it.

Another volley of shots. One of the soldiers was shouting through a megaphone, his words blurred and indistinct. The children in the bus were laughing with relief, hugging each other. Including me and Anna – how embarrassing is that? As soon as we realised we sat straight and still next to each other.

The bus powered forwards, then slammed to a halt in front of the second gate as the first one began to slide slowly closed again as soon as we passed through.

It was like going through an airlock. The gates clanged shut behind us and a soldier tapped on the remains of the side window. The driver pulled a little lever and the door opened to let the soldier in to check the driver's paperwork. He looked along the bus and gave us a cheery wave. One of the girls waved back. Her face was stained with tears.

The second gate opened and the driver brought the bus slowly inside the compound. I could see his shoulders moving as he breathed heavily with relief. The door was still open, the soldier standing on the step, like he was riding shotgun on a stagecoach in an old Western.

'You'll be OK now, folks,' he shouted as he showed the driver where to park. 'Safest place in DC in here.' He grinned, as if proud of how many teeth he'd got left – though it wasn't that many. Then he jumped off the moving bus and jogged back to the closing gates.

'It might be the safest place in Washington,' Anna said quietly. 'But it's here the world ends.'

'Might end,' I said, hoping that just saying it would make me feel better. But her words had sent a shiver through me more bitingly cold than the draught from the broken bus window. 'We'll stop them. We'll shut down the experiments.'

Anna turned to look at me, her lips sort of bunched up like they are when she's thinking. 'These experiments shouldn't be happening at all. Not at this time in history.' She hesitated, then dismissed the term. 'You know what I mean.'

'I know what you mean,' I agreed. 'So we don't just stop them, we find out how they started and sort that out too. And another thing . . .'

'Yes?'

The bus had stopped and the driver was yelling at us all to get off. He said something about unloading luggage and I wondered what the boy

I'd replaced had packed and whether it would fit me. I could see a flicker behind Anna's eyes too as she probably had a similar thought.

'If this compound is kept so safe, guarded by the army and surrounded by electric fences and machine-gun posts and God knows what to keep out that hungry mob . . .' I said.

'Yes?'

We lined up behind the other kids to get whatever baggage was left when they'd reclaimed theirs.

'And it's some sort of scientific lab where they just happen to have accidentally developed time travel . . .'

'They're getting close,' Anna said. 'They haven't done it yet. But, yes?'

I took the last but one bag and glanced at the name tag. It said Mandy, so I handed it to Anna.

'Then why do they need the children?' I helped myself to the last bag and smiled at the driver watching us from the other end of the bus. He glowered back at me. 'Not that I'm complaining, because it gives us a way of getting in without anyone wondering who we are or why we're here.'

'It's a good question,' Anna said thoughtfully as we followed the other kids towards a large steel security door with a soldier on guard outside. It was like a miniature version of the gates we'd just come through.

'I only ask,' I told her as we went through, 'because it sort of affects us now. Given we're here and they think we're with the other kids.'

Anna didn't answer. I couldn't see her expression, because her face was thrown into shadow as the heavy door slammed shut behind us. Trapping us inside the building.

It used to be a school, before the riots and the first breakaway states. We got taken to our dormitories – separate for boys and girls, obviously – to dump our stuff, then down to the old school hall for a pep talk.

As well as the eight of us from the bus, there were about half a dozen other kids finishing a pretty meagre lunch. I'd got talking to the other three boys in the dorm. There was Jeff, who was sixteen, built like a tank and about as bright. He was wearing jeans and battered trainers and a pale blue sweatshirt with a black logo of a pouncing tiger on it. I wondered what it meant, but decided Jeff probably didn't even know himself. Assuming it meant anything.

Spencer was a swotty-looking eleven-year-old with glasses. Ray was fourteen, kept very quiet, a tall, lean African-American. We sat together at one of the two long tables that ran up the length of the enormous hall. A different table from where the other kids were eating. The girls came and sat further along the same table as us.

I looked at Anna and was about to suggest she introduce herself and the other girls when the double doors at the back of the hall banged open. Three people walked in – two men and a woman. The men walked purposefully past us, the woman slightly more hesitantly, smiling nervously as she passed.

There was a raised area at the far end of the room – probably the stage from when it was a school hall. The three of them climbed up on to it and looked back down at us. Conversations died away. The kids who hadn't been on the bus were obviously old hands and knew the drill. They were paying careful attention. In fact, we were all paying careful attention. All except Jeff, who was still laughing at a joke he'd just got from ages ago.

His snorting laughter came to an abrupt halt as he realised the three adults were looking at him.

'Thank you,' one of the two men said. He was tall and thin, wearing a long white lab coat. His hair was thinning and turning to grey and his nose was so narrow and pronounced it looked like a beak. 'My name is Dr Kustler and I'm in charge of this facility. I'd like to welcome our new guests and introduce my colleagues here.'

He paused to survey the huge room, as if it was full of people and not just the fourteen of us. 'Compound Delta is essentially a research facility,' he went on, 'and what we do here is sensitive and secret. But in these difficult times I think it is important that we do all we can to plan for the future. Which is why we allow – in fact,' he corrected himself, 'positively encourage students to join us for brief placements. My scientific staff is largely engaged on our research work, but we can all spare time to give lessons and lectures and impart knowledge.'

Jeff's frown was turning to something close to horror at the realisation that this was still a school after all. 'Oh, great,' he said, sounding anything but enthusiastic.

'Knowledge,' Kustler went on, 'and also discipline.' He fixed Jeff with a beaky stare until the boy looked away, embarrassed into silence again.

'Now,' Kustler said, 'my most key staff, at least so far as you are concerned, would like to introduce themselves. Then we will leave our newcomers to get acquainted with the old hands and learn some of the detail of what goes on here and how we expect you all to behave.' He stepped aside and motioned for the woman to take her turn.

She was short and broad, with a round face. Maybe it was always a bit red, or maybe she didn't like talking in public. Her voice was quieter and less assured and we had to strain to hear everything she said. 'My name is Margery Dorril,' she said. 'I am the housekeeper here, which means I'm responsible for keeping the place running in domestic terms. The catering, cleaning, all that sort of thing falls to me. And I am also responsible for your welfare and for looking after you generally. I know it's a shock to be taken away from the place you had come to regard as your home, so we'll do our best to make sure your stay here is enjoyable and not too much of a wrench. It isn't for long, after all.' Her voice dropped away, as did her gaze, and she looked down at the floor. 'And then you'll be going home again.' She glanced nervously at Kustler. 'Thank you.'

Kustler nodded, as if to say she'd done all right.

The third person didn't wait to be told. He stepped forward and started right in. He was a broad-shouldered man, middle-aged and tough-looking. He wore a suit but he stood like a soldier. When he started, 'Now, listen up,' I almost laughed out loud.

'Now, listen up. As well as the domestic side of things, Dr Kustler mentioned discipline. And that's something we set a lot of store by. With good reason. You saw the mob outside. That's what happens if you let yourself go, if you give in to chaos, if you don't stick to the rules. That's why I'm here – I'm in charge of discipline. My name is Alford, but you will call me "sir" just like the soldiers do. Any trouble – I deal with it.

Any problems – they come to me. And if you are one of the problems, or you get into trouble, then you will get no sympathy. Got it?'

There were murmurs from the other table.

'That's good,' Alford said, as if we'd all shouted back, 'Sir – yes, sir!' like in the films. 'You play fair by me and do what's expected of you, and you'll find it's not so tough. Let's all do the best we can and obey orders and we'll get along just fine.'

He took a smart step backwards.

'Yes, good. Thank you,' Kustler said, before leading the way down from the stage. He smiled reassuringly as he passed our table again. Then he paused, right beside me. He gave a slight frown and tapped his chin with his finger. 'What did you say your name was?' he asked, pointing the finger suddenly at Jeff.

Jeff looked round to see who he meant. I said he wasn't too quick. 'Jeff,' he said when he'd worked it out. 'Jeff Ziegler.' Then, as an afterthought, 'Sir.'

'Of course.' Kustler nodded and smiled. 'Perhaps you'd like to come with me, Mr Ziegler. I need to have a quick word about something.'

Jeff looked at me and I shrugged. I could almost feel Alford standing close by, so I reckoned Jeff had better go with Kustler like he'd asked. The boy untangled himself clumsily from the bench beside the table and followed the adults from the room.

The doors closed and there was silence.

'Guess he'll get roasted for laughing in class,' Ray said.

The kids from the other table were coming over. One of them heard Ray – a girl of fifteen with hair so red it almost glowed. 'That isn't why Kustler wants him,' she said.

'How do you know?' Spencer asked. His voice was nasal and wheedling. Irritating.

It certainly seemed to irritate the redhead. '*Because*,' she told him. 'That's why.'

'They might say we're here to learn, to take classes and study,' one of the boys said. 'But that ain't it.'

'What, then?' Anna asked. She and the girls from the bus were shuffling down the benches to join us, all clustered round the middle of the long table.

The redhead gave a snort of derision. 'We

24

don't know why we're here,' she said. 'We ain't figured that out yet. But there were a dozen of us last week and now's there's six.'

'Fourteen, you mean,' one of the girls with Anna said.

'That's right,' Spencer put in. 'Six of you, eight of us.'

'Seven of you,' the redhead said. She sounded sad rather than irritated now. She looked straight at me, as if I was the one who was most likely to understand what she was telling us. 'Like I said, we don't know what they want with us. But I do know one thing. That guy Jeff who just left with Kustler . . .'

'Yes?' I prompted her.

She sighed before telling us: 'We ain't never gonna see him again.'

They gave us a tired-looking salad each for a late lunch, and we got to know each other. The red-haired girl was Amy. She introduced the other kids who'd been there for a while. She referred to herself and them as the survivors, which didn't exactly make the confidence swell . . . I pushed the salad round my plate, not feeling very hungry.

The other girls were Florence and Pam. Florence was thin and sour-mouthed, with braided hair. I could think of a more polite way of saying it, but Pam was large. She was tall and, let's face it, fat. But she had a good smile and a cheerful round face.

The boys were Julio (dark skin, dark hair, no

26

visible emotion), Davie (nervous and freckled) and PJ (lanky, with spots – loads of spots). No one asked what PJ stood for. Pyjamas, maybe. Pyjamas Smith – that'd be a good name.

I introduced myself, Ray and Spencer. Anna introduced herself and the other new girls – Becca (big teeth), Santini (lots of make-up, despite being only eleven) and Kate (long plaits and train-track braces on her teeth, both top and bottom).

There were no formal lessons or anything that afternoon. From what Amy told us, there wasn't much education going on at all. It was all just an excuse for us being there. But why, no one knew. We spent some time looking round the facility.

'We're only allowed in certain places,' Pam said. 'Anywhere off-limits has an "Authorised Personnel Only" sign. Anywhere else is OK.'

'But don't let the General catch you where you ain't supposed to be,' Davie warned us.

'The General?' Kate asked.

'Alford,' Julio said. 'He's not really a general. He's like a major or something. But we call him the General. Something Chrissy made up. She was funny.' He turned away. 'Chrissy ain't with us any more.'

'How long have you all been here?' I asked.

'Varies,' Amy said with a shrug. 'I've been here nearly a month now, along with PJ. Julio and Florence were here before me.'

'Six weeks,' Julio said. 'Give or take.'

'And Pam and I got here last week,' Davie added. 'We're the new kids. Or were till you lot showed up.'

There was a gym, though nothing much in it – just an empty space marked out for basketball with a few weights and a set of climbing bars. Loads of empty classrooms. The old staff room from when it was a school had been made into a sort of common room for us – with easy chairs that should have been retired years ago and desks where we could work. The wood was scarred and pitted and people had scratched their names and spilled ink on it. There was a TV too, but Pam told us it only got the 'government channels'.

'We can do without that propaganda crud,' Becca said. She had a mobile phone – tiny and pink. But there was no signal.

'We think they suppress it somehow,' Amy explained. 'Don't want us netting the blogs and

28

finding out what's really going on out there.'

'Or calling for help,' Julio said quietly.

Having explored the few, boring areas where we were allowed, we chatted in the common room until six. Then it was time for tea back in the hall – a vegetable stew that looked more tired than the salad. The chunks of potato had bags under the eyes.

Amy was right about Jeff. There was still no sign of him when Mrs Dorril appeared in the common room at nine and announced it was time we all went to bed.

'What happened to Jeff?' Anna asked. She's never afraid to be the one to make a point or get awkward.

Mrs Dorril looked uncomfortable and her face reddened again. 'He, er, he had to leave, I'm afraid.'

'He went back to the orphanage?' I asked.

Mrs Dorril nodded quickly.

'Why?' I asked, as much to see what she'd say as because I thought I'd actually find out.

'Dr Kustler was not impressed with his attitude.'

'Do lots of people have to leave?' Anna asked.

29

'If Dr Kustler isn't impressed with their attitude?'

Amy was staring intently at Anna – maybe trying to warn her off. Or maybe surprised at the fact someone was actually asking.

'It happens,' Mrs Dorril said. 'Now, I want you all in your dormitories, please. It's been a long day for you newcomers.'

'Perhaps we can send Jeff a letter or something,' Anna said levelly. 'He's a good friend. Just to see he's all right.'

'I could email him,' Becca said. She showed Mrs Dorril her pink phone. 'Only I can't get a signal. I thought everywhere was networked in now.'

'We'll discuss it tomorrow. Now – bed.'

We all trooped out. I was last to leave the room, apart from Mrs Dorril. I looked back from the doorway and saw she was leaning on one of the tables, staring down at it. Her shoulders were trembling. I pulled the door closed and followed the other boys up to our dorm.

Like everything else, the dormitories were too big. I mean, seven boys in a room with about forty beds. It was as much like an old hospital as a school, I thought. Each of us had a cubicle. The beds were arranged along both sides of the long room, each partitioned off by thin wooden walls that reached about three-quarters of the way to the ceiling.

You could grab the top and pull yourself up to look over into the next cubicle if you wanted. But the wood was warped and knots had fallen out, so if you did want to keep watch on next door, it was easier just to peer through. I found my cubicle easily enough – it had my bag on the bed, ready to be unpacked. Well, I say my bag. It actually belonged to a boy called Mason Laing, but he didn't need it because he was frozen in time outside his orphanage. Caught between the split seconds, where no one but me and Anna could ever see him. Mason wore pyjamas that were pale yellow and he hadn't even packed a book.

The front of the cubicle didn't have a door, or a wall. There was a curtain you could drag across. I pulled mine back and forth experimentally, hearing it scrape on the metal rail above. The fabric was rough and faded and over twenty-three years old. I could tell.

Getting bored with that, I wandered the length of the room to see where everyone else was. Ray had drawn his curtain across, but he was the only one. Jeff's bag was on a bed near the end of dormitory, which was a bit of a give away that he hadn't really left. I guessed the 'General' would give someone three degrees of hell over it when he found out.

At the end of the room there were two small bathrooms, neither of which I fancied giving my business. Then there was a toilet, which was worse, and stairs down to the floor below and up to the dormitory above. I could hear laughing and giggling and whispering coming from upstairs, so no prizes for guessing where the girls were.

As well as a bed, there were a cupboard and a small sink in my cubicle. So I closed my curtain and had a wash. I stuck my head back round the curtain and shouted a goodnight, punctuated by an exaggerated yawn, then climbed into bed. Yes, fully clothed.

But if anyone glanced in they'd see I was snuggled up and asleep. I closed my eyes and speeded time up. No way was I going to lie there bored and with nothing to read for the four and a half hours until two in the morning. I was taking the quick route. A minute at the most.

🕐 THURSDAY 18TH MARCH 2021

Even though it was two o'clock in the morning, there were still people up and about. Patrolling guards, workaholic scientists, undercover Time Runners . . .

Anna was there at exactly two, as we'd agreed, and she'd stopped time. We wanted to be able to explore without being seen or interrupted, and we wanted to explore all the places we weren't supposed to go. The fact they'd been kind enough to put up notices that said 'Authorised Personnel Only' and actually meant 'Secret Stuff This Way' was a big help.

They did seem to have gone over the top, though. Even the kitchens were authorised personnel only.

I said to Anna, 'I think they should do a set of "*Really* Authorised Personnel Only" as well, to give us more of a clue.'

She smiled at that. Nice smile.

'Or "Chefs Only". Let's try this way,' Anna suggested as we left the darkened kitchens. 'She might be a clue.' She pointed to a white-coated woman – scientist or lab assistant – caught in a split second between steps in the corridor. 'She must know where she's going.'

'Or coming from,' I said. 'Maybe she's after a sandwich.'

Anna looked at me sideways. 'You've tried the food here,' she said. 'You really think she wants more of it?'

'Fair point.'

Apart from our voices, there was complete silence. But as I spoke, I thought I heard something else. A faint sound from behind us, a scuffling like someone dragging their feet. I turned quickly, but there was nothing. Or almost nothing.

Was that shadow in the alcove darker than it had been? I peered at it, waiting to see if someone – or something – moved. I could make out a vague shape, like a hunched figure hiding in the darkness of the alcove . . . I took a step towards it, but Anna was already heading the other way. I hesitated a moment, then followed her, glancing back over my shoulder. But nothing moved and there was no sound.

There was a security door at the end of the corridor. It opened by swiping a plastic card with a magnetic strip, which I had to explain to Anna. Of course, there was nothing like this in the 1940s. But once I told her it was like having a key, she understood. We could have gone back and borrowed the white-coated woman's badge. She'd never have known. But it was easier to wind on till she got there and opened the door for us. Then we froze things again, with the door open and the woman still holding her card.

'This is more like it,' Anna said as we entered a large laboratory.

There was electronic equipment everywhere and several more white-coated scientists standing by a large metal archway. It looked like one of those ironwork trellis frames you get in a big garden that people grow things over. Only instead of roses or honeysuckle, this was wreathed with wires and cables that led back to the equipment.

'Time experiments?' I said.

'Oh, you're just guessing.' But Anna was grinning – bingo!

'So what now? Do we start time going again and see what they're up to? There's no sign of the great Dr Kustler,' I noted.

Anna had walked all round the archway, careful not to go through it, even though time – and therefore everything else – was turned off. Behind the archway was another corridor. From where she was now standing, Anna could see partway along it. She paused and frowned.

I followed her as she went to the corridor. I could see now that one side wall was made of glass. It was a viewing gallery, looking into a series of small rooms. I guess it was between fifteen and twenty metres long and ended in a bare concrete wall. The half-dozen narrow rooms along the corridor looked rather like the cubicles up in the dormitory. Bed, sink, a cupboard in the corner which I realised might be a toilet . . . There was a heavy steel door at the back of the little room. Like a prison cell.

The first couple were empty. Then we came to one that had a cot instead of a bed and I could see a baby lying inside, eyes closed in peaceful sleep.

'Childcare for the staff?' I said.

Anna didn't answer. She moved on to the next

36

one. Where an old lady was curled up in the bed. She had kicked the covers off and little wrinkled feet were sticking out of her nightgown. Her face was even more wrinkled, and her hair was long and white. She was sucking her thumb.

'Weird,' Anna said.

'Not childcare,' I admitted. 'Now it's granny flats.'

The next of the cells had a man in it. Like the baby and the old woman, he was on the bed. But he was lying on top of the covers and his eyes were wide open, staring back at us. Not that he could see us, of course, as time was at a standstill. He was propped up on the pillows and his lined face was a pale mask of fear. Even through the glass I could see a tracery of tears down his cheeks. He was completely bald, the top of his head peppered with liver spots.

But that wasn't the oddest thing. The oddest thing was that he was wearing a pale blue sweatshirt with a black logo on it. A leaping tiger, just like Jeff's. And jeans. And battered trainers.

'I don't like this,' Anna said quietly beside me.

'Me neither.' I swallowed. 'Those clothes . . .'

But Anna wasn't looking. She was tapping her

time dial in annoyance. 'There's something . . .'

A sound from back down the corridor, from the lab, made her stop. She looked at me, eyes widening. We could hear voices, the clatter of someone putting something down. The door slamming shut behind the woman who had unknowingly let us in. Time was starting up again.

I quickly looked at my own time dial. Twisted, adjusted, thumped it. Nothing.

'Maybe it's the experiments, causing some sort of interference,' Anna whispered.

'We can't get caught here,' I said. 'God knows what they'll do to us.'

'I think I can guess,' Anna said gravely. She was looking past me, into the cell.

And something slammed into the glass right behind my head. I jumped, my heart missing a beat as I leaped back and turned.

The old man was standing on the other side of the glass wall, thumping on it with his gnarled, withered hands. He must have been eighty at least and he could barely stand up on his own. But his eyes were fixed on me with determination and purpose.

'Hey, man!' He was probably shouting to be

heard through the glass. 'Hey, man, you gotta help me. You gotta get me out of here.'

'We'd better go,' I said, grabbing Anna's arm. 'Before someone hears him.'

'You can't just leave me,' the old man shouted. 'Jamie!'

At the sound of my name I froze – like time had stopped again. I turned slowly back towards the glass, realising what Anna had already known.

A shadow fell across the end of the corridor as someone approached from the lab, cutting us off.

'You gotta help me, Jamie,' the old man said. Another tear was rolling down a cracked cheek. 'I dunno what they've done, but you must get me out of here. Don't you understand – you must help. You can't leave me. We're friends. Come on, Jamie – can't you see?'

And I could see. I could see that the old man in front of me had actually only lived for sixteen years. I could see the leaping tiger on his shirt. I could see the fear in his pale, moist eyes.

I could see that despite being old and withered, it was Jeff.

'Someone's coming,' Anna hissed. Like I didn't know. 'My dial doesn't work.' Like I didn't know that either.

But I was staring at the old man Jeff had become, I was feeling cold and empty. Time still surprises and frightens me. I looked at Jeff and I saw the old age I would never have and which had come on him in hours rather than years.

I didn't mean to do it. These things sometimes just happen and maybe I'll learn to control them. I'm getting there, slowly. Jeff's hand was pressed hard against the window. His wrinkled palm flattened out by the pressure. I pressed my own hand against his – or rather, against the other side of the window, really just to reassure him.

A shadow fell into the narrow gallery, stretching towards us across the floor as someone approached. Another moment and they'd see us.

The glass shattered. Or so it seemed. In fact, its time hurtled backwards. In a second, it was a thousand years ago for that pane of unbreakable safety glass. I felt it go, felt the power running through me. And I felt Jeff's hand warm against mine, trembling and afraid. The glass was a pile of sand at my feet.

Without a word, I grabbed Anna and bundled her through the opening that now led into Jeff's small cell. I squeezed Jeff's arm gently, saying nothing but hoping he could feel my sympathy. His eyes were pale and watery and unfocused as he tried to take it all in.

'Under the bed,' Anna whispered.

It was like being back in the bus, except this time I could see what was happening. I peeped out from under the metal-framed bed, aware of Anna lying close beside me. We had only just made it.

One of the white-coated scientists was standing by the hole where the window used to be. He was staring, open-mouthed. Jeff was laughing – his whole frail body shaking as the laughter turned to a fit of coughing. He walked slowly over and sat down on the bed.

The scientist was shouting, yelling for his colleagues to come and look.

'What's happened?' another man asked, as astonished as the first.

'Looks like it's disintegrated,' the woman we'd seen in the corridor said.

'And they're supposed to be experts on how time works,' Anna breathed.

That made me smile, despite the fear that they'd look under the bed and find us.

'You'd better move Ziegler to another observation room,' the second man said. 'No.' He held out his arm to stop them just stepping into the room. 'Go round the back. Best not disturb the scene.' He made it sound like they were investigating a crime. Time crime.

There was a pause for about a minute, then we heard the scrape of bolts and the creak of the heavy door being swung open. I tried to twist round to see, but couldn't do it without sticking my head out of cover. So I listened as hard as I could.

'Come on, Ziegler,' the woman was saying. The bed moved slightly as Jeff stood up. Footsteps.

'I'll find Dr Kustler,' the man still at the window – where the window had been – said. He shook his head as he looked down at the sand spread across the corridor, then turned and walked away.

I waited another minute, then risked putting my head out and looking all round. The cell was empty; the scientist out in the corridor had gone. Beside me, Anna was pulling herself out from under the bed.

'They'll be back soon,' she said quietly. 'Come on.'

'Not that way,' I said as she headed back towards the window. 'That just leads back to the lab and there are sure to be people there.'

'We can't stay here.'

I pointed to the heavy metal door, now standing open after they'd taken Jeff to another cell.

'I still can't get my dial to work,' Anna whispered as we stepped cautiously out of the cell. 'Lucky your powers don't seem to be affected.'

'No guarantee they'll work again,' I said. But I was aware that – this time – I had managed to control them, at least to an extent. I had managed to funnel the power that came to me and make it do what I consciously wanted rather than just what I instinctively felt.

We were in another corridor, one that ran along the other side of the row of cells, or observation rooms as the scientist had called them. I couldn't be sure which way they'd taken Jeff, so I took Anna's hand and together we ran quickly and quietly to the nearest end of the corridor. It opened into a large office area. A door led back into the main lab and I could hear Kustler's voice, though I couldn't make out what he was saying. There were desks with computers on them, and other equipment like printers and photocopiers. The desks were partitioned off with low screens. Some of the screens had papers pinned up on them – year planners, photos, memos, a few cartoons.

'We need to get back to the dorm,' I whispered.

'Or escape,' Anna said. 'You saw what happened to Jeff.'

'You think that can happen to us?' It wasn't something that had occurred to me, but it was an unpleasant thought.

'I'd rather not find out.'

That went for both of us. It was bad enough being trapped as a twelve-year-old. Imagine being trapped as an old man. Or, I thought as I remembered the cot in the other cell, a baby ... Who had that been? Would they become themselves again in the years ahead or grow into someone quite different?

The voices in the lab were getting fainter and I realised that the people – including Kustler – were leaving. We edged closer to the door and saw that everyone was now clustered round the end of the corridor past the cells.

'Examining the damage,' Anna said.

'Puzzling over the evidence,' I agreed. 'Reckon we can slip past?'

'Reckon we have to try. There's no other way out that we've seen.'

'Still the door to deal with,' I said. But there was no sign of a badge-reader on this side. Once in, maybe you could leave without using a badge. Was it worth a try?

I didn't get the chance to decide, as Anna was already on her way, walking quickly and quietly across the lab. I followed, trying to make it look as if I was supposed to be there, in case anyone saw us or caught a glimpse of movement. Something furtive and nervous might catch their attention, where just another person walking out of the room might not.

My chest convulsed briefly as Anna tugged at the door – and nothing happened. Then she pulled again, harder, and dragged it open.

'Stop mucking about,' I whispered as soon as we were through. The corridor beyond was mercifully empty.

'It was heavy,' she protested with a glare. 'Thanks for helping.'

'Back to the dorms,' I suggested. 'We need to get our dials working again before we can do anything much else.'

It was strange and nerve-racking to have to creep about as if we weren't supposed to be there. I wasn't used to it, wasn't used to not being able to just stop everything and everyone and do what I wanted without anyone else knowing. Anna was nervous too, I could tell.

But there was also a bit of a buzz to it. The flow of adrenaline, or something. Excitement. After all, what was the worst they could do to us if we were caught, I wondered as we reached the stairs leading up to the dormitories. Then I remembered the feel of Jeff's dry, wrinkled hand against mine and I tiptoed all the more cautiously after Anna.

Breakfast was dry bread and old cheese, and my time dial still wasn't working, which was a worry. But if it was being affected by the experiments there probably wasn't a lot Anna or I could do about it, not for the moment anyway. We all sat at one of the long tables in the hall and Julio told us that food came in once a week, or maybe once every two weeks. It arrived in huge armoured trucks that the soldiers had to go out and protect so the starving people outside didn't rip them apart.

'Food . . . such as it is,' Ray said.

'I remember milk,' Florence said. 'You know – from cows.'

'Comes from goats too,' Spencer told her.

She ignored him and he went back to pulling

his bread roll into tiny bits. No one seemed very hungry.

Mrs Dorril was nervously pacing the room, as if to make sure none of us wandered off. Maybe she always did this. Or maybe the strange events at Jeff's secret cell had made them cautious.

'Mr Alford is coming to see us,' she announced when we'd all finished. 'So I'd like you all to wait here, please.'

'Going to send someone else home?' Amy asked. Her voiced was laced with sarcasm. 'Who's the lucky one this time?'

'I don't know what Mr Alford has in mind.'

'Isn't he a general, not a mister?' Santini asked. 'He acts like a general.'

'Just mister. You can call him "sir".'

'I heard he was a general,' Ray said. 'Heard he was in the army or something, isn't that right?'

Mrs Dorril looked even more uneasy than usual as Ray stared at her. He was standing up, much taller than Mrs Dorril, and even down the length of the table it must have been intimidating.

'I don't know if Mr Alford has been in the army,' she admitted, turning away. 'He was in the Secret Service, but that was a long time ago and he doesn't like to speak of it. Now, sit down, please, Ray.'

Ray sat down, taking his time and stretching out his long legs under the table. 'Doesn't like to talk about it?' he said quietly, grinning. 'Hey, that's good to know.'

We chatted for a bit while we waited and Amy challenged us 'newbies' to a basketball match in the gym in the afternoon. It sounded like fun – a bit of normality in a crazy world.

'Is that like netball?' Anna asked me quietly.

'Think so,' I told her. 'Only boys play too, so it's less vicious.'

'Thanks.'

'And needs more skill.'

She tilted her head to one side. 'So why do boys play?'

I was saved from having to think of an answer as Alford arrived at that point. He strode into the room, shouting, 'Now, listen up, team.'

'Here comes Coach,' Ray said, and we all laughed.

Alford stared at us, his lips curling into an almost-smile. 'That's good,' he said loudly. 'Humour. Good safety valve.'

'Do we need a safety valve?' I asked. The words came out a bit louder than I intended and, as Alford turned towards me, I immediately regretted them.

'We all need a safety valve.' He was serious again.

'Even Secret Service men?' Ray asked, all innocent. 'You think they need a safety valve, Mr Alford, sir?'

Alford's expression didn't change. And he was still staring right at me. 'Even generals,' he said. 'Or so I hear tell.'

'Hey – are you a general?' PJ asked.

'Far as you're concerned, I'm the Lord God Almighty and don't you forget it.' Alford turned and looked at each and every one of us in turn as he spoke. 'Things ain't easy here. I know that. I know you're confused and you're wondering what's going on. Let me tell you guys, that goes for us adults too. Here and all across America.' He looked at me, then at Anna. 'All across the world, most likely.'

'So?' Amy said. But her voice lacked the earlier confidence.

'So, what happens here is for the good of us

all. It might not always seem like it, and there's hardship and problems. And if I could spare any one of you one second of that hardship, believe me I would.'

'Right,' Ray muttered.

But I was more convinced. It seemed to me that Alford was trying to tell us something. Trying to tell us that what was happening here wasn't his fault – and that under the right circumstances he might be a friend. But maybe I was totally wrong. And before I had a chance to decide whether he was potential friend or probable foe, I was slumped forward over the table like I'd been thumped in the gut.

I could feel breakfast fighting to put in a reappearance and struggled to keep it down.

'You all right?' Anna said quickly. She was worried – all the more worried because she could guess what was happening. Some sort of problem with time and I could feel it. Something terrible was about to happen. Any moment . . .

'Jamie?' Mrs Dorril was all sympathy and concern.

I managed to straighten up. I could see Pam frowning at me, wondering what my problem was. 'Got a bit of bread stuck in the throat or something,' I said.

'You'd better get it unstuck,' Alford said, 'because we have a visitor. Dr Kustler will be here in a moment and he's got someone with him for you to meet. So I want best behaviour, I want civility and no talking back.'

'Who is it?' Becca asked, impressed already.

'Mr Knight is responsible for the financial health of this facility. Without him you wouldn't be here and neither would any of the rest of us.'

'And you want us to be civil?' Ray said.

'You'd better be,' Alford told him. 'Dr Kustler's looking for a volunteer, someone to help out with a little experiment.'

Anna and I exchanged looks. 'OK?' she mouthed, and I nodded back. Just about.

'Here he is now.'

We all twisted round on the benches to see as the door opened and Dr Kustler came in. But neither Anna nor I spared him more than the briefest glance. He held the door open for his companion.

But it wasn't a man who came through the door.

The grotesque, gargoyle-like creature ran past Kustler and stood watching us, a dry tongue licking stone-cracked lips. The wings folded across its back shivered as it swayed from side to side in anticipation. A skitter.

And it was followed by another, then a third. They arranged themselves inside the doorway, watching hungrily and making a scratching, clicking sound that was unpleasantly like laughter.

Kustler, of course, had not seen them. Any more than Alford or Mrs Dorril, or any of the other children had. I'd felt something dreadful was about to happen. And here it was.

Kustler nodded and smiled to the man who came into the room behind him, following the skitters. He was tall and thin, wearing a dark suit and carrying a silver-topped cane. Alford had called him Mr Knight, but I knew his real name.

Darkling Midnight – the most fearsome of the Dark Runners, and our bitter enemy. Someone who revelled in chaos and destruction. He paused just inside the hall and the skitters scampered round him like attentive children expecting a treat. More were scampering into the room behind him, flickering in and out of my perception. He patted one gently on the head, knowing that no one else could see it – he was just moving his hand.

No one except Anna and me. He looked right at us, smiling as if he had expected us to be there. Kustler was introducing him as Mr Knight, but I barely heard what the man was saying.

Then Midnight spoke – his voice rich and dark and dripping with self-confidence.

'You were about to ask for volunteers, Leo,' he said to Kustler. He was looking from me to Anna and back again. Smiling horribly. 'I really don't think there's any need. We seem to have just exactly the young people we need, right here.'

'We're not going anywhere with *you*,' I said.

Anna was close beside me, pale-faced.

'Really, young man?' Midnight was charm itself. He smiled at Kustler and nodded amiably at Alford and Mrs Dorril. 'Kids today . . .' He shook his head as if he had no idea why I was reacting so vehemently. He'd affected an American drawl which made him sound even more laid-back and relaxed about things than usual.

'Show some respect to Mr Knight,' Alford barked.

'Indeed,' Kustler agreed. 'We all owe a great deal to Mr Knight. Literally.'

'*We* owe him nothing,' Anna said. 'And he knows it.'

55

Midnight looked offended. As if he couldn't understand why two children he'd never seen before should take against him like this. I was struggling to think what to do. It wasn't like I could tell Kustler, 'Don't listen to him, he's an evil maniac from outside time who's using you to wreak havoc and chaos across the world in every period of history – somehow.'

So I kept quiet and waited to see what Midnight would do. Anna was frantically twisting her time dial, while keeping it out of sight under the table. But Midnight has a way of stopping them working. Perhaps it wasn't Kustler's time experiments that had interfered with our time dials the night before – but Midnight. He must have known we were here.

'I think our volunteers have selected themselves,' Midnight said. His skitters were watching us malevolently through their little red eyes. 'What are your names?' he asked me and Anna. Like he didn't know.

'Mickey and Minnie Mouse,' I told him.

Ray laughed. But he stopped the moment Midnight looked at him.

'Why do you want to know?' Amy demanded.

I could see in her eyes that he scared her too, and she probably didn't know why.

Midnight sighed and shook his head, as if it was all very sad. 'I have seen Dr Kustler's meticulous and very detailed records of the children who have been through the educational exchange programme here,' he said.

'Is that what it is?' Amy retorted.

'I'm learning lots,' Ray said. But he said it very quietly.

'That's good to hear ... Ray,' Midnight told him. 'And thanks for the input, Amy.'

Neither of them could meet his stare. Amy looked down at the table. Ray turned to PJ and shrugged.

Midnight walked slowly over towards us, skitters darting in and out from behind him and hissing at the oblivious children as they approached. 'Now, Mickey and Minnie – or should I say Jamie and Anna? That's right, isn't it?'

'You know it is,' Anna said.

'What do you want?' I demanded. 'What are you doing here? Apart from causing trouble.' The other kids were watching me and Anna in astonishment. Even Amy seemed surprised at how we were talking to the important Mr Knight.

'So rude,' Midnight said, amused. 'And we've only just met. But I have to say, from the files, you two seem the very best candidates for Dr Kustler's next experiment. Oh, don't worry,' he went on in a tone of voice that made me feel a convulsion of fear, 'there's nothing to be afraid of. It's all very straightforward. Very safe. Just a few simple tests. And when they're over, well, we'll send you home.'

'You mean back to the orphanage?' Anna said.

'What else could I mean? Of course, we can't let you spoil the fun for your friends by telling them about the tests afterwards. That might upset any future tests they might themselves help with, isn't that right, Leo?' He honoured Kustler with a brief glance, as if giving him permission to agree.

'That's correct,' Kustler agreed. 'You'd best say goodbye to your pals now. Mrs Dorril will arrange for your belongings to be packed up.'

'Of course,' Mrs Dorril said. She was dabbing her nose with a hanky. When she thought no one was watching, she dabbed at her eyes too.

'But,' she said, voice shaking, 'Jamie is ill. I think he may be coming down with something.'

'That's right,' Anna said quickly. She ignored my frown and shake of the head. 'You can't run tests on Jamie – he's not well.'

'I'm sure that won't affect the results,' Midnight said. 'And it's all very simple and straightforward.'

'I'm fine,' I said. No way was I letting them take Anna and leave me. Or take any of the others.

'Can't you postpone these tests?' Mrs Dorril said, her face glowing as she blushed. 'Just until Jamie is feeling better,' she added quickly as Kustler fixed her with an icy stare.

'The boy did seem to suffer some sort of attack just now,' Alford said. He met Kustler's gaze. 'I'd have to agree with Mrs Dorril here.'

'Leave Jamie,' Anna announced. 'I'll come with you. No protest, I'll help. But leave Jamie.'

I couldn't believe she was saying this. 'No! We both go, or neither of us. I'm fine. I just caught my breath, that's all. We both go,' I told her.

'Tell you what,' Kustler said, sounding very reasonable and calm. 'We'll take the girl first. Come back for the boy later. OK?'

Mrs Dorril bit her lip and nodded.

Alford turned away.

Midnight smiled and walked over to where Anna and I were sitting.

I was breathing heavily, angry and afraid. I grabbed Anna's arm and held it tight with both hands. 'She's not going!'

'Oh yes, she is,' Midnight said quietly. He gently took Anna's other arm to help her to her feet. Ignoring my hold on her. Not even watching as one of the skitters flexed its long, stone-like fingers, then sank sharp talons into the backs of my hands. I struggled to ignore the pain, my eyes watering so much I could hardly see. But I could feel my fingers being prised away from Anna's arm.

'Leave me,' she said quietly. 'You can't stop him. At least this way . . .'

I had to let go or my fingers would have snapped. I didn't hear any more of what Anna said as my whole body shook with a sudden uncontrollable sob.

A hand patted my shoulder. A human hand, apparently sympathetic. Midnight.

'Don't worry,' he said quietly, so only I could

hear. All trace of his American accent was gone. 'I'll be back for you soon.'

I couldn't bear to watch as he and Anna walked away. The skitters snapped their teeth and laughed in front of me till Midnight had reached the door. Then they turned and scampered after their master.

The door slammed shut behind Kustler, Midnight and Anna.

Alford sat down, looking suddenly old and tired. Florence reached across the table to put her hand over mine. Mrs Dorril clamped her handkerchief to her face and hurried from the room.

I went to my dormitory cubicle and lay on the bed. Just until I could decide what to do. I couldn't leave Anna to fend for herself. But what *could* I do? Barging into the lab and confronting Kustler would do no good – not with Midnight and the skitters there. OK, so I could still use my own developing powers, even with my time dial not working. But despite my success with the window, there was no guarantee that I could properly control those powers, or that they were even close to a match for Midnight's.

I felt useless. Worse than useless – Anna had gone willingly to protect me, at least for a while. If it weren't for me, she might have fought and got away. The idea that *I* could get away, abandon Anna, never entered my mind. She'd bought me a little time and there had to be some way to use it.

Without making a conscious decision, I had got off the bed and was walking along the dormitory. Our mission here was to stop the time experiments. I also had to rescue Anna before she got either aged like Jeff or regressed to a baby. Or something worse. And I wasn't going to achieve either of those things by lying on my bed feeling sorry for myself. The place to do it was the lab – where the equipment for the experiments was, where Anna had been taken.

Kustler and Midnight were both there too, but I'd just have to deal with that – somehow. I was quaking inside. It was like being sent to the head teacher – you don't want to go, but you know you have to. If you don't, then things will be even worse. Every step was heavier than the last, every breath seemed to do less good than the previous one . . . Until, at last, I was in the corridor leading to the lab.

The door was shut and without a badge I couldn't get in. I'd passed a couple of soldiers further back, and I could hear people bashing pans and talking in the kitchen. I could go back and ask someone to let me through. Assuming their badges would work.

But I wasn't sure I could trust myself to take the time, to walk away and still come back. So instead, I swallowed, took a deep breath and knocked loudly on the door.

There was a small square window in the door, with lines of wire set into the glass. I couldn't see anything much through it. The window was too small to show more than a bit of wall. Then a face appeared – Kustler. He looked back at me with a puzzled frown. Then the door clicked open and I went through.

I felt better as soon as I was inside. Partly because now there was no going back – like getting on stage in the school play. But mostly because I could see Anna – safe and well – standing beside the metal archway. She sighed and glared, and I shrugged back. I could see, though, that she was trying not to smile with relief.

'I'm delighted you could join us,' Midnight said. He was close to Anna. Several skitters flapped their wings threateningly, but I ignored them. Midnight waved his hand impatiently and they backed off, looking bored and frustrated. 'Feeling better?'

'I'll be a lot better when you let Anna go and tell us what you're up to.' I tried to sound confident and defiant. Maybe I did. If so, it was a good act.

But it was an act that failed to impress Midnight. 'Oh, I don't think that's a very good idea,' he said, twirling his cane. 'Not when Dr Kustler is getting such interesting results.'

'It doesn't work on me,' Anna said quickly. 'This stuff has no effect.'

Kustler was at a control panel close to the metal archway. 'I can't understand it,' he said, shaking his head. 'We should be getting something. I thought by linking the ...' His voice tailed off. 'I'll have to get Wilson to check the linkages again.'

'There's nothing wrong with them,' Midnight said quietly.

'Then why is nothing happening?' Kustler

demanded. He thumped the panel. 'With the new changes, she should travel back in time and appear here five minutes ago.'

'But she didn't,' Midnight said, amused.

'So it doesn't work,' I said.

Kustler glanced at me, and I realised that the fact he was speaking so openly about his plans and intentions meant he wasn't planning on letting either of us go afterwards. 'If it doesn't work, then her personal time stream should be affected. Like the others. Her life would speed up and she'd age, or run backwards so she becomes a little child.'

'But she doesn't,' Midnight said. He slapped the silver end of his cane into the palm of his hand. 'It's intriguing, isn't it?' He looked from me to Anna as he spoke. 'Almost as if this girl had some sort of special relationship with time. As if it ignores her.'

'As if,' Anna said.

'Why not try it yourself and see what happens?' I said. For the moment things seemed calm and, apart from the presence of Midnight himself, Anna and I didn't appear to be in danger.

Kustler glared at me. 'I don't think that's a

good idea,' he said. 'Not again.' He took a step towards me and I instinctively took a step back. I didn't like the look he was giving me – solemn and thoughtful, his hands thrust deep into the pockets of his long white coat. I guessed he'd had enough conversations with Midnight to know something about how time works. But he must have been a bit surprised that I was able to join in the conversation. Maybe he resented that, because he added, 'But putting someone else through the temporal gateway *is* a very good idea.'

'He means this archway thing,' Anna said.

That was pretty obvious. 'Thanks,' I told her. 'What makes you think I want to help you?' I asked Kustler.

'What makes you think you have a choice?' He pulled his right hand from his coat pocket and I saw he was holding a pistol. He gestured with it for me to walk through the archway.

'You'll be fine,' Anna said.

'Oh yeah?' But what if I wasn't fine? Would I come out the other side wrinkled and frail? Or would I be on all fours, sucking my thumb and wanting my mummy?

There was only one person here who knew for sure what would happen. I looked at Midnight. He met my gaze and nodded. I didn't trust him, but, like Kustler said, I had no choice.

I expected to feel something, like a tingling or an electric shock or ... Well, *anything*. I walked through the archway, aware of Kustler's eyes watching me closely. And ... nothing.

'I don't understand it,' Kustler cried in anger and frustration. 'I just don't understand this at all.' The gun was still pointing at me and he rubbed at his forehead with his free hand.

Midnight was smiling. He pointed his cane at Kustler. 'And hold it there,' he said in a quiet but firm voice.

Kustler froze, suddenly absolutely still, handkerchief pressed to forehead and gun pointed at me. Midnight walked slowly all round him, as if to make sure he hadn't missed anything.

'Good,' he announced, as he walked slowly over to Anna and me. He walked through the archway, without hesitation. 'How very quaint,' he murmured as he came through with no ill effect. 'Now, I think we should have a little talk, my friends.'

'We're no friends of yours,' I told him.

'How can you think that?' Anna demanded.

Midnight seemed mortified. The skitters were chittering together in the corner of the room, as if they understood our anxiety even though their master did not.

'But I do so much for you,' Midnight said.

'Like stuffing us through dangerous time experiments,' I suggested.

'Jamie, Jamie, Jamie . . .' He was shaking his head sympathetically. 'I just want what's best for you.'

'I bet.'

'Of course I do. I want you to work for me, and for my colleagues in the Dark Assembly.'

'He isn't for sale,' Anna said. She took my arm and held on protectively.

'Everyone is for sale,' Midnight countered. 'Everyone has their price. Jamie might not do anything to get put back into time, to get his old life back. But he'd do anything for you to get yours.'

I felt almost sick at his words. I'd never thought about it before, but he was right. More than anything – more than I wanted to go home, to be *real* again, I wanted the same for Anna.

She rarely talked about her life before she was lost, before she fell through one of the cracks in time. But I knew from the little she did say how much she missed it. How much she wanted to be a normal child growing up, with a family, and loved, just as I did.

Midnight had his head tilted to one side, as if to gauge our reactions better. 'And you'd do anything for Jamie,' he said to Anna. 'Just – anything. Right?'

She didn't answer. I tried not to think about that.

'Not convinced?' Midnight asked. 'Then let's take Dr Leo Kustler here.' He turned to inspect the motionless scientist. 'He'd do anything, well almost anything, to stop what's happening to his country. He'd sacrifice the children of today to prevent yesterday from ever happening. That's why he's here. He'd give his own life – and maybe he will – to stop President Carlton ever falling to his death. Like so many, he sees that as the defining moment. The instant when America started its own decline. The country fell with its president. And Kustler will sacrifice anything to stop that from happening.'

'Is that what all this is about?' Anna asked. She's quicker than me on so many things. 'He wants to go back and save the president.'

'He thinks that will save his country,' Midnight confirmed, smirking at the thought. 'I don't know if that's more naïve than thinking he can actually do it.'

'If you know he can't do it, why are you helping him?' I asked.

While everything was stopped, maybe Anna and I could get away. We'd still have to close down Kustler's experiments somehow, but one thing at a time.

'You know you can't get back into real time and reclaim your lost lives,' Midnight said. 'But it doesn't stop you from hoping, or from trying to see if you could find a way.'

'That's different,' Anna said.

'Is it really? We all have our dreams. And,' Midnight said, leaning towards us and watching carefully for our reactions, 'Sellwood went home.'

Neither of us responded to that. But I'm sure Midnight saw the reactions he was expecting. Norman Sellwood had worked for Midnight during one of our previous encounters. Sellwood was lost like me and Anna, taken out of time itself. Even his own wife didn't know who he was. Yet Midnight had kept his promise to the man – somehow he had put him right back where he came from. Just like he'd never been lost at all.

'You know how Carlton died?' Midnight asked. 'Just out of interest, do you know what Kustler is trying to prevent?'

'There were rumours it was an assassination by some terrorist group,' Anna replied. 'Law and order broke down. America became frightened, and it was every man for himself. Gun law, looting, political manoeuvring to see who the next president would be ... The economy collapsed.'

'The vice-president was *so* ineffective,' Midnight agreed with obvious relish. 'Not up to the job at all, I'm afraid. And dead from a heart attack within the month.'

He swung his cane in an arc and the air split. It was like he was peeling back one layer to reveal the scene hidden beneath. A view of the top of a high building. A helicopter was coming in to land on top of the building. Tiny figures were running towards it.

'A routine flight from the Judson Building helipad to the emergency crisis talks at the Torvald Center in New York,' Midnight said. 'Out of the stairwell, across to the helicopter. What they might call a cakewalk.' He smiled thinly as he watched the tiny figures hastening across the top of the building – president, staff, Secret Service. 'The agent in charge is a man called Alford, by the way. That might help explain things to you.'

It did. But I wasn't really listening. I was watching the tiny figures as they disappeared from view behind the landing helicopter. Then one of the figures emerged from behind it – hurrying, running, sprinting for his life.

'Here he comes.' Midnight licked his lips as he watched. Another figure followed President Carlton. We only caught a glimpse – but it looked more like a large dog than anything. A bulky, hunched creature, hurrying on all fours across the roof. A guard dog maybe? After whatever was chasing the president? They were only visible for an instant, then they were both hidden by a line of men in dark suits running across between us and the president.

A shout.

A figure falling from the edge of the building – arms scrabbling in the air, legs going like he was still running. The president.

'Tragic.' Midnight lowered his cane and the scene faded. 'An accident, of course.'

Neither Anna nor I said anything. I could see she was thinking the same as me. If it was an accident, why was the president running? If it was an accident, what was the thing that had been hurrying after him? Did they know what was going to happen?

If it was an accident, why – just as Midnight dismissed the scene – could we hear the angry drumbeat of gunfire?

'And anyway,' Midnight was saying, 'you need to bear in mind that if I cannot persuade Jamie to come and work for me, the next best thing would be for him to work for no one.'

Anna stepped in front of me. 'Don't you dare touch him.'

Midnight laughed. 'Oh, dear me, young lady. You do misunderstand. Why would I want to harm him? What good would that do me? I have, I confess, come to respect and even like you both. So, if he won't work for me, I might as well put him back into time, like Sellwood. Then he'd be no threat to me at all. You too, if you'd like.'

'You can't do that,' I said. But I didn't believe my own words. I'd seen him do it.

'It's easy enough,' Midnight said lightly. 'Though I would need – did need – some equipment. A small component called a time synchronisation coordinator, not that the name matters. Something that Kustler will have to develop in the next few days to get his equipment working how he wants. So he can travel through time rather than have time travel through him. He doesn't want to get younger, he wants to go back. So he needs the coordinator. And what he learns from you two will lead him to that.'

'We won't help him,' I said. 'We came here to stop his experiments, not make them work.'

Midnight smiled, amused by the dilemma he was giving us. 'If you stop his experiments, you really will seal your own fate. Sellwood was a special case. I took him out of time in such a way that I could push him back into it with barely a ripple. Even so, it was too much for the coordinator I had. It burned out in the process. So I need another, more powerful coordinator if I am to do it again. Lost really will be forever. Unless you let Kustler invent the component I need to save you both.'

'We don't believe you,' Anna said slowly.

But I knew she did believe him, just as I did. If we wanted to go home, if we wanted to save ourselves – if I wanted to save Anna – then we had to let Midnight win.

There was no sense of time slowly getting going once more. It didn't gather speed like a car pulling away. It was just 'on' again in a moment.

Kustler did all sorts of tests on us. He took blood samples, checked our heart rates and how much we sweated after riding an exercise bike. He shone lights in our eyes and he checked our reaction rates with a board where you have to press a button when it lights up.

After several hours, we were allowed a short break. On the way back to the common room, Anna and I agreed we didn't have much choice. We had to let Midnight continue with his plan – at least for now.

'We help him till he works out how to build this coordinator thing,' I said.

'Then we get back to the mission,' Anna agreed.

'At least we now know why the experiments are so advanced.'

'Midnight.'

'Right.'

Kate was alone in the common room. She'd been crying and made little attempt to hide it as we came in.

'Are you all right?' Anna asked at once.

The girl nodded and sniffed. She attempted a smile, the metal of her braces glinting.

'Where's everyone else?' I asked. Had she skipped off lessons?

'They've gone.' She sniffed again. 'Amy said we have to get out, before they take us all and do awful things – experiments.'

'She's probably right,' I said, slumping down in a battered old armchair.

'Hang on,' Anna said. 'What do you mean, "gone"?'

'Gone,' Kate repeated. 'Left. They went to the main gate, said they were going to leave the compound and go somewhere else.'

Anna and I looked at each other. 'Where?' Anna asked.

Kate shook her head. 'Didn't say.'

'But the guards won't let them leave,' I told her.

'Spencer said that. PJ said they could force their way out.'

'There are soldiers – with guns.' Anna was shaking her head in disbelief.

'Ray said they wouldn't shoot children.'

I hoped he was right. 'Why did you stay here?' I asked.

'Where would I go?' she replied quietly, looking away.

'We have to stop them,' I said.

But Anna wasn't convinced. 'Do we?'

'What do you mean?'

'What if Amy and Ray and the others are right? What if they're better off away from here.' She fixed me with her intense green eyes. 'We saw what happened to Jeff.'

'Don't remind me.' She was right, though. It was impossible to know what to do for the best. But as it turned out, we didn't have to make a decision.

Alford came for us. Kustler was ready to

run some more tests, and since Alford had two grim-faced soldiers with him, we didn't argue. Though we would have done if we'd known what Kustler was intending . . .

There were two tables set up in the laboratory. They were padded and raised slightly at one end, a little like the dentist's chair when it stretches out and lies you down. Kustler motioned for us each to lie on one of the tables. With him was a woman in white overalls. She was wearing a surgical mask over the lower half of her face. Her eyes looked both frightened and sad at the same time.

Anna and I lay down, expecting more of the same sort of treatment we'd had before. I thought he'd shine bright lights in our eyes or take our pulse or check the colour of our tongues.

As soon as we were settled, Kustler nodded to the woman. Kustler was by my table, the woman by Anna's. They each reached underneath and pulled out long, dark straps.

'Hey, wait a minute.' I tried to sit up, but Kustler pushed me firmly back down. The strap was across my chest, clicked into place on the other side of the table as Kustler leaned over me. More straps – across my legs and waist. I could see Anna struggling with the woman.

'I'm sorry,' the woman was saying. 'I'm so sorry.'

It looked as if Anna might manage to push her away, to undo the single strap across her chest and get up. But having finished with me, Kustler turned and pushed Anna viciously down on to the table, holding her while the woman – the nurse – fixed the other straps.

I was straining and fighting, trying first to break the straps or their fastenings. Then trying to wriggle my arms or hands free. But there was no way I was going to manage it.

Kustler was breathing heavily as he stepped back, and I saw Anna lying as trapped as I was. On the operating table.

'Right,' Kustler said, snapping on thin, flesh-coloured latex gloves. 'I think we're about ready for the anaesthetic.' He leaned over me again, face close to mine, eyes shining madly. Behind him, the nurse was holding up a syringe. She flicked it to get rid of any air bubbles. A drop of colourless liquid appeared at the end of the needle.

Kustler was pushing up my sleeve. I cringed and tried to pull away. No good. He had the syringe now, the sharp tip of the needle pricked against my arm. Kustler smiled reassuringly and I knew he was about to push the syringe home. I waited for the numbness to spread down my arm and into the rest of me.

But nothing happened.

Kustler remained exactly where he was, about to inject the anaesthetic. The nurse's frightened-sad expression did not flicker.

Had I done it? Had I managed to stop time? I dared to think that I had. Anna thought so too. She was grinning with relief as she continued to struggle against the straps. We were still tied down, but I reckoned I could age the straps so they disintegrated, or even just shift the operating table to a point in time where the straps simply weren't fastened.

Then the door swung open and I realised that I could do nothing. That I had done nothing.

'I was afraid you might start without me,' Midnight said. He took in the frozen scene at a glance. 'I see that I am just in time.'

Several skitters were clustered round the table,

peering at me through malevolent little red eyes and clicking their forked tongues against their stony lips with amusement.

'Just get us out of here,' Anna demanded. 'You've made your point.'

Midnight was all sympathy. 'Oh, if only I could.' If he hadn't been holding his silver-topped cane, he might have been wringing his hands together in mock sympathy. 'But you of all people know the dangers of changing the course of events, changing history. I really shouldn't do it.'

'You do it all the time,' I told him through gritted teeth.

Midnight smiled, the act over. 'Yes,' he agreed. 'But I shouldn't.'

'Just do it,' Anna shouted. 'Undo these straps and get us away from that maniac.'

'Oh, please – he's a distinguished and very highly regarded scientist. And he is about, with your help, to make the most exciting discovery of his career. You can't deny him that.' Midnight sounded as if he was describing Einstein to schoolkids. 'Scientists, as part of the process of discovery, have to make sacrifices, you know.'

He gave a short laugh. 'It's just unfortunate that you happen to be one of those sacrifices.' He slapped his hand down on the top of the table close to Anna's head, making her flinch. 'On the altar of science,' he said.

'All right.' I struggled to sound calm and keep my voice level. 'You've had your fun.' I broke off as I felt a sudden pain in my arm. I had pulled away from the needle as soon as I could, but now it jabbed suddenly into my skin before stopping again.

'Oh, not yet I haven't. The fun is about to start.'

Midnight did not seem to have noticed. He did not seem to have consciously allowed time to start up again for an instant. How had that happened, I wondered? There was a glimmer of an idea lurking in my mind. Midnight was able to stop us from manipulating time. Maybe I had the same power, to a degree at least. Maybe somehow, just now, I had for a moment blocked Midnight's control over time.

I didn't waste long wondering about it, though. It would do me no good at all to allow Kustler to carry on jabbing the anaesthetic into my arm. But maybe, sometime in the future ... If I had a future.

Midnight was leaning comfortably against a filing cabinet. 'There is just one small change I think we need to make,' he said. He snapped his fingers and time did start up again. My eyes were watering and my heart thumping. The needle pressed into my upper arm, forcing its way through the skin and searching for a vein ...

Then he stopped, as Midnight said from behind him, 'Just one small suggestion.'

Kustler stepped back, holding the syringe up. 'I didn't hear you come in, Mr Knight.'

'You were busy, I didn't like to interrupt. But I do wonder if perhaps ...'

'Yes?'

'The boy knows something, I'm sure. I think he could be persuaded to cooperate ...' Midnight raised his eyebrows – to be sure I understood what he meant. Which was 'Come and work for me', and I wasn't going to do it.

'I still think an internal examination would be extremely useful.'

'Oh, I agree.' Midnight was still looking at

me rather than at Kustler. 'I just think it might be beneficial if you started with the girl.'

Anna pulled away at that, straining at the straps but without success. I was shouting at Kustler as he turned towards Anna, cursing Midnight. I've no idea what I was yelling – screaming – but the nurse's eyes were even more frightened above her mask. I was rolling back and forth in a last, desperate effort to break free. There was some give in the straps, but not nearly enough.

Even over my shouts I could hear the laughter of the skitters. Kustler's mock-soothing words as he raised the syringe. Midnight's calm entreaties to me to help and everything would be all right.

And I knew I would have to agree. The syringe needle caught the light as Kustler prepared to thrust it into Anna's arm.

Then – gunfire.

Shouts from outside. Running feet. The door to the lab bursting open.

Alford was there, flanked by several soldiers. 'We have a breach,' he said. His face was almost white.

Kustler turned, frowning. 'What are you talking about?'

'Those kids – some of them tried to get out. They opened the main gates.'

'Why didn't you stop them?' Kustler demanded.

'You expect us to shoot at *kids*?' the soldier closest to Alford said. 'Kill children?'

Kustler looked down at the syringe he was holding, then back at Alford and the soldiers. But I don't think the irony struck him. There was more gunfire now from outside. More shouting and yelling. 'A breach? You mean – there are people actually inside the compound?'

'We're trying to hold them back,' Alford told him. 'Minimal force, but there will be casualties.'

'They're after food,' the soldier said. 'That and protection. Shelter. Blankets. Whatever they can find.'

'Get them out,' Kustler shouted. He was shaking with anger. 'I won't have this facility overrun with criminals.'

'They're not criminals,' Alford said quietly. 'They're victims. They're the people we are trying to help.'

But Kustler ignored him. 'Clear them out –

all of them,' he demanded. 'Shoot them if you have to.'

Neither Alford nor the soldier replied. They exchanged glances, and then Alford turned and walked quickly from the room. The soldier gestured to his colleagues and they followed.

They were gone only a few moments. Only long enough for Kustler to turn back towards Anna. Then one of the soldiers hurtled back through the door and crashed to the floor. The door was sagging, lock and hinge broken. Gunshots very close by. Alford shouting something. There was a single shot – so loud it echoed inside my ears.

A mass of people erupted into the lab. The first of them were at once ripping open drawers, searching through papers, opening cupboards. Some running for the office area beyond. There were men, women and children – all ages, races ... Clothes in tatters, faces drawn and eyes now glinting with something between hope and greed. All tired and emaciated and angry.

Kustler lunged at Anna. But the nurse suddenly ran forward and thrust him aside. One of the buckles holding the straps on my table snapped open as people pushed past.

Then everything was still and silent. Midnight was in the midst of it all, walking slowly towards me as I struggled to reach another strap, fingers clawing desperately at the catch. I could see Kustler falling – caught halfway to the floor and hanging impossibly, staring accusingly at the nurse, the syringe clasped tight. For the first time, frozen in split second, the nurse did not look frightened.

'If you want something doing properly ...' Midnight said with a sigh. He reached out and prised the syringe from Kustler's hand. He turned towards Anna. 'Let me know if you change your mind, won't you?'

The skitters clustered round, trying to see what their master was up to in among the mass of people. I could just see Anna's frightened face, staring at me – pleading as I scrabbled at the straps still holding me down. The syringe held above her, ready to come down into her immobile arm ...

'Do something!' Anna yelled.

Midnight brought the syringe down like a knife.

Struggling to be free of the straps, there was only one thing I could do.

The mass of people came to sudden and noisy life as I blocked Midnight's control over time. Midnight's hand was knocked away as they jostled and fought and pushed and shoved. Someone – an old man – was undoing Anna's straps. I finally managed to break free of mine and jumped off the table.

Midnight was being carried with a tide of people towards the door to the office. They seemed to think there would be more chance of finding food or whatever they were after in there. His cane clattered to the floor and was kicked away. I saw Midnight's pale features contorted in fury as he struggled against the tide.

Then the skitters were rushing in. A blur of movement, like air shimmering on a hot day. People were being thrust aside and pushed away without knowing what was going on. Invisible hands clawed at them, fighting to get to Midnight. Soon he was safe in a protective island of calm among the mass of the moving people.

But I wasn't watching. I was helping Anna off the table. The nurse was there too, holding Anna's elbow and murmuring encouragement.

'I'm fine,' Anna protested. She had to shout above the sound of the people pushing through the lab into the office beyond.

I saw Kustler stagger from the lab in the other direction, into the corridor. He was holding his head in his hands, moving uncertainly, stooped and bent over so his lab coat trailed across the floor. He looked as if he'd taken a bashing and I wasn't at all sad about that. The nurse hesitated, then muttered something to us which I didn't catch before hurrying after Kustler.

There was no sign of Midnight.

From the office came the sound of shots.

A burst of staccato machine-gun fire like a road mender's drill. The sound of shouting and movement stopped. I went cold as I wondered what might be happening to the people who had just pushed past. Then Alford's voice rang out as the sound of the people grew again.

'Listen up – all of you. You shouldn't be here and you can't stay. But I understand. Really I do.'

He was yelling to be heard. Anna and I moved towards the door so we could see. Alford was standing on a table, holding the gun he must have fired to get their attention. There were several nervous-looking soldiers close behind him. A wisp of smoke curled from the end of the gun.

'You want food? Blankets? We'll do what we can. If you all just calm down. The gates are closed again. No one else is coming in. There's no rush. You're safe here for now. We'll give you what food we have and you can eat it here inside the compound, out by the gates. Then you have to leave. Like I said, we'll try to find you blankets, whatever else we can.'

'We're staying here, mister,' a woman shouted.

'No. I'm sorry – but that just isn't possible.'

There was an eruption of angry shouting. Alford pressed down on the air with his hands to calm the crowd again.

'You can't stay here. That's the deal. You get food, then you leave. We have work to do, work that can maybe help you all.'

'What sort of deal is that?' someone called out. 'Do you know what it's like outside? We're dying out there!'

Alford fired a single shot into the ragged hole already torn in the ceiling above him. 'It's all I can offer,' he said in the silence that followed. 'Accept it and get fed before you leave. Or else we'll throw you out by force. Without food.'

There was angry muttering. But the mood of the crowd had changed. I could tell they'd accept. Whether they'd still agree to leave peacefully after they'd eaten was another matter. But that was Alford's problem.

'Where's Midnight got to?' I wondered out loud.

'Never mind him.' Anna was heading for the door out to the corridor.

'Where are we going?' I asked her.

The door was hanging in its frame, jammed against the floor and twisted on its hinge.

'To find Amy and Ray and the others,' she said, as if it was obvious.

I guess it should have been. They were our friends – or as close as we were going to get – and I'd just forgotten all about them. What had happened when the crowd forced its way into the compound? Had Amy and the others escaped? Been forced back inside? Been stopped by the guards? Trampled under foot?

My head was filled with possibilities as we hurried along the corridor. Most of them not good. The lights flickered and went out. The whole place was suddenly washed in a dull red as emergency lighting switched in.

'Power cut?' I wondered

'They don't have power cuts in America,' Anna said. 'They have outages and brown-outs and jargon like that. And they have them all the time now, or so Senex said. Since they stopped getting oil from the Middle East.'

'Spare me the history,' I muttered.

As soon as I said it I hoped Anna hadn't heard. She was as worried as I was. Maybe more. Girls worry more than boys. Or so it seems. Though I reckoned I was worried enough for the both us right then.

Somewhere, in the semi-darkness, we'd taken a wrong turn. We were in a section of corridor neither of us knew. A door on one side opened into what had been a classroom. Desks and tables were lined up. There was a white board at the end of the room with a teacher's table in front of it. A chair lay where it had fallen over. Grey evening night shone through holes in the thin curtains pulled across the grubby mesh-covered windows and fought with the red of the emergency lights.

'Let's go back,' Anna said.

'Yeah.'

We both turned. Both hesitated as we heard the sounds from further along the corridor. A cry of fear and pain. Long and sharp, cut off suddenly as it rose in volume. A woman screaming for help. Then nothing. Anna's eyes were wide in the red of the corridor. Neither of us moved.

A door slammed shut – somewhere in front of us. I grabbed Anna's hand and we hurried on.

There was someone in the corridor with us. I could make out the dark silhouette in the blood-red light. A broad-shouldered, slightly squat figure. A man? Hunched, almost like an ape. Powerful arms hanging by the figure's sides as it lurched away from us. I stopped, holding Anna back, sensing danger.

'Who is it?' she whispered.

I shook my head – no idea. 'We so have to get our dials working again,' I told her.

The creature in front of us turned, perhaps at the sound of our hushed voices. It hissed, ragged teeth catching what light there was. Eyes as dark as sin, glinting malevolently. Skin covered with matted fur and dark hair. Where had it come from – what was it? The creature slashed the air between us with a sudden rake of its paw, and I stopped trying to work things out and concentrated on just being terrified. We backed slowly away and it looked for a moment as if the thing was going to follow us.

But then it turned abruptly and lurched off down the corridor.

'What is that thing?' Anna said.

'No idea. Not friendly, though.'

95

'That scream . . .' Anna had hold of my hand still and tugged me forwards. 'Come on.'

I held back. 'You're not thinking of chasing it, are you?'

'Someone cried out. Someone's in trouble.' She let go of my hand and ran on ahead.

'So long as it isn't us,' I called after her.

There was a door, just by where we'd seen the ape-like creature. The door we'd heard slam shut? It seemed likely. Anna had her hand on the handle. She turned to look at me, eyes asking, 'Shall I?'

I nodded, biting my lower lip and ready to grab Anna, turn and run.

Anna twisted the handle and pushed. The door swung open slowly. Another classroom. The curtains were open in here, allowing the grey of the evening to mingle with the red of the emergency lights. And of the blood.

The woman was lying in the middle of the room. Desks had been pushed aside, chairs toppled. She was face down, arm outstretched. A surgical mask lay close to her body. Even without it, I recognised the woman from the lab – the frightened nurse who had helped Anna and then left when the crowd of rioters pushed its way in.

Now she was here, in an abandoned classroom, face down in a pool of blood. Dead. If our time dials – or my own growing powers – had been working, we could have replayed the events in that room and seen how she died.

But then, did we really need to? Whatever the grotesque creature was that we'd seen in the corridor, it had done this. Violent, savage, deadly . . .

'Was it a skitter?' I asked. My voice was dry and throaty.

Anna shook her head. 'Don't think so. Bigger, more savage.' She glanced nervously back towards the door, afraid the thing might reappear. 'And it was in real time.'

'How do you know that?'

I heard her take a deep, ragged breath before she answered. 'The woman was aware of it. She saw what attacked her.'

'She cried out,' I realised. 'She screamed. So it's real. That thing really exists.'

'We have to stop it,' Anna said. Like me, she found it difficult to look away from the horrific sight of the woman's body for more than a few seconds. 'This has to be something to do with the experiments. And we have to stop them, before there are any more deaths.'

A bright torchlight cut through the gloom and illuminated the body. In the sterile white light it was even worse and we both turned quickly away.

Kustler was standing just behind us, and behind him were three soldiers.

'You're right,' he said. 'We can't have any more deaths.' He shone the torch full in my face as he waved the soldiers forward. 'But now we've caught the culprits, we don't have to worry about that, do we?'

My arms were twisted up behind my back before I had a chance to answer him. Anna cried out in pain as she got the same treatment. The soldiers dragged us towards the door.

Kustler tracked us with the torch. 'Murderers!'

CHAPTER EIGHT

'Let them go.' Alford was standing in the doorway.

The soldier holding me glanced at Kustler, then back at Alford, unsure who to obey.

'Let them go,' Alford repeated, and the soldier let go of my arms. Anna too was free, and we stood between the calm Alford and angry Kustler.

'They're murderers,' Kustler protested.

'We didn't do it,' I said.

Kustler snorted, though whether in disbelief or anger I couldn't tell.

'That's right,' Anna said. 'We heard her cry out and we came to see what the matter was.'

'Sounds plausible to me,' Alford said.

'We caught them red-handed,' cried Kustler.

'And they would be red-handed.' Alford nodded at the body behind Kustler. 'So let's see.' He stepped forward and grabbed one of my hands, pulling it forward. Then the other. He then repeated the process with Anna.

'What are you doing?' Kustler demanded. His lab coat was ripped and stained, and I reckoned part of why he was so angry was because the mob had given him a hard time. Not that he was a bundle of joy and happiness before they broke in and trashed the place.

'If they're the murderers, then, like you said, they'd be covered in blood,' Alford told him. 'Look at her, look at her injuries. You really think these kids could do that? And even if they could, they'd be covered in blood.'

He turned to the soldiers. 'There's a murderer loose. Maybe more than one. Shut down this area, nobody in or out. Everyone confined to quarters.' He looked back at Anna and me. 'Or common room. Those kids that are left.'

I wondered if that was just us and Kate.

'And I want this room sealed, as soon as we're out. Move!' Alford barked.

The soldiers moved. Leaving Alford and Kustler alone with us. And the body of the nurse.

'What did you see?' Alford asked, his voice surprisingly quiet. Kustler took a step towards us.

'A figure,' I said slowly, wondering how much to tell them.

'We didn't see it clearly,' Anna added. 'Just a shape in the corridor.'

'We heard the nurse cry out.' I shrugged. 'The figure left the room, we came in to see who'd screamed.'

'How do you know she's a nurse?' Alford asked.

'Syringes, needles, surgical mask,' Anna told Alford. 'Take your pick.'

Alford was frowning at that. 'We need to have a talk,' he told Kustler. 'Later.' Maybe Alford was more of an ally than we'd thought.

'This figure you saw,' Alford went on.

'That they *say* they saw,' Kustler interrupted.

Alford ignored him. 'This figure you saw – anything unusual about it? What sort of height, weight? Male or female? You see its face?'

Anna glanced at me before replying. 'It was big. We didn't see it too clearly. Didn't really see the face. But . . .' She broke off, considering. 'There was something odd about it.'

'Odd?'

'It was sort of hunched over,' I said. 'So its arms reached right down, almost to the floor.'

Alford nodded. He looked suddenly pale. 'Lot of hair?' he asked.

'Yes. Now you mention it.'

Alford sighed, his expression grim and anxious. 'Just like last time,' he said to Kustler. 'Still think these kids did it?'

Kustler pushed past us. 'I have things to do,' he snapped, and disappeared into the blood-red corridor.

'What do you mean, "last time"?' I asked Alford.

'There was another death, another murder. A few days ago. Before you two got here.' He led us out of the room and closed the door. 'One murder is bad enough. Two is worse. But two unconnected murders committed a few days apart by different people for different reasons, each leaving the body in the same horrific state?' He shook his head. 'I don't buy that.'

*

The lights and power were back on by the time we got to the common room. Kate was sitting in one of the armchairs, knees drawn up so her chin was resting on them. Florence was sprawled on a sofa, looking as if she'd been dragged through a hedge backwards – or an angry, hungry crowd of rioters. Her hair was all over the place, her face streaked with dirt and her clothes a mess.

The only other person in the room was Spencer. He looked scared and, judging by the angry gash on one side of his face and the fact that a lens of his glasses was cracked and the frames bent, he probably had good reason.

'Total waste of time,' Florence told us when Alford was gone.

'We could have been killed,' Spencer said. His voice was shaking. 'Those people are mad. Crazy.'

'Hungry,' Florence said quietly.

'What happened to the others?' I asked.

'PJ got away, I think,' Florence said. 'Alford says that Amy's in hospital. Some army place a few blocks away. With electric fences and armoured cars. She'll be OK.'

'Broken arm,' Spencer muttered. 'Not too serious.'

'Dunno about the others,' Florence went on. 'Didn't see Ray at all once we got outside.'

'The guards let you out?' Kate asked.

'Like Ray said, they couldn't shoot us,' Florence told her. 'Amy kept them talking and arguing while Ray and Julio got the gates open. Only opened them a crack.'

'But the crazies outside did the rest,' Spencer said. 'I got knocked down in the rush as they came in. Soldiers shouting, then gunfire.' He shook his head. 'I never made it out of the compound.'

'So what now?' Anna asked them.

'We stay here,' Spencer said glumly. 'Where it's safe.'

'Safe?' Florence snapped. 'Are you kidding? After what's happened to Chrissy and Jeff and the others? And now there's this murder.'

'Second murder,' I said.

They all stared at me.

'Looks like they managed to cover up the first one,' Anna said.

'Oh, my God,' Florence wiped her hand across

her face, smearing the dirt. 'We *so* have to get out of here.'

'Haven't done too well so far,' Kate told her.

'At least I tried,' Florence snapped back.

'Which makes you a better person how exactly? Not like you achieved anything, is it?'

'Oy!' I yelled, suddenly angry as well as frustrated and frightened. 'Stop it, both of you. This isn't going to help.'

They subsided into silence. Both girls looked away. Florence pulled at her torn clothes in an effort to rearrange them. Kate rubbed at the frayed fabric on the arm of her chair.

Spencer turned the telly on. 'News,' he complained. 'That's all there is now. And they never tell you anything. Food riots in Los Angeles, Texas on fire, people dead in some cop bust in Milwaukie. The usual.'

We watched anyway. There was a soldier standing outside the open door, occasionally looking in at us. So it wasn't like we were going anywhere.

The screen showed a man giving a speech. The caption under the grainy, flickering picture read: 'Senator Miles Georgeson'.

He was an impressive speaker, even with the sound and picture breaking up every few seconds. Passionate and determined.

'We have to stop treating them as criminals,' he was saying, 'and seeing them as victims. We are all victims. And it's up to us to help ourselves. The world outside doesn't care. The Seventh Cavalry ain't coming. There's just us. Just America. And our greatest enemy is ourselves. So let's get the troops out there, yes. Let's put more cops on the streets, yes. Let's bring back our boys from the Gulf and Asia and put them in our own cities, on our own street corners and in every neighbourhood. But let us do it not to round up the disaffected, not to shoot looters, not to impose law and order. Let's put them there to help. To distribute food, to rebuild homes, to provide shelter. To restore our pride and our respect.'

Someone was shouting at him. The camera didn't show who it was. We didn't hear what they said. But Senator Georgeson responded at once, leaning forward and talking directly to the camera.

'You think that sounds like the Third World?

Let me tell you something, that's because we're *living* in the Third World. And if you think this once great country can go on the way things are now and come out the other side, you ain't living in any real world at all – first, second, third or otherwise.'

The picture screwed sideways as he was speaking. At that point, it gave up altogether, rolling and distorting. The sound cut out.

The soldier on guard at the door had come into the room to watch with us. 'Useless,' he said, and went to turn the television off. 'Satellites are all gone to hell. But Georgeson,' he went on as he returned to the door, 'now he's the only guy in this whole mess of a country who talks any sense at all these days. Sooner they make him president, the better.'

'Who's the president now?' I asked.

The soldier paused in the doorway. 'Who knows?' Half his mouth twisted into an ironic smile. 'Who cares?'

'We have to get out of here,' I said to Anna quietly. 'We have to do something.'

'Like what?'

'Like get our time dials working.'

'How?' she said.

'You tell me. Is it Kustler's experiments that's interfering with them or is it Midnight?'

'Maybe both.'

'We could wreck his equipment,' I suggested. 'Probably should. Before it wrecks us. Alford wasn't impressed, but he won't stop that maniac for long.'

'You mean Kustler or Midnight?' She was almost smiling, which was a good sign.

'Maybe both,' I said, replaying her own words to her.

'Let's get out of here, then,' Anna said.

'With a guard on the door?'

'No problem.'

I love it when Anna gets all efficient and sorts things out. It's great to watch. She went and sat on the sofa close to the other kids and told them that we – me and Anna – had to get out and sort some stuff. She was vague enough to give nothing away but conveyed the impression it was important and would help them too.

'We came here on purpose,' she said. 'To sort things out. We took the places of two others who were supposed to come.'

'Mason and Mandy,' Kate said.

Spencer nodded. 'That's right. They were coming too, but then when we got to the bus – it was you guys. Who are you?'

'Never mind that for now. Just help us get out of this room.'

'But how?' Spencer said.

Florence sighed. 'Wimp,' she said, standing up. 'Leave it to me.'

She walked to the door and shouted at the soldier from close up, 'I need to go the bathroom and I ain't going out there alone with no murderer on the loose, thank you.'

The soldier blinked under the onslaught. He reached for his radio. 'I'll get someone to escort you, miss.'

Florence stamped her foot – actually stamped it. Like an angry toddler. 'I need the bathroom and I need it right now.' She gave him a second before adding, 'Or do I have to go here?'

'No, miss. Er – you'd better . . .' He swallowed and stepped into the room. 'Stay here, right?' Then he hurried off after Florence, who was already halfway down the corridor.

'Right,' I echoed.

'You want us to come with you?' Kate asked. 'Can we help?'

I looked at Anna, shaking my head just slightly. 'Best not,' she said.

'You sure?' Kate asked.

Spencer just looked relieved. Wimp was right. And I was fine about that – he was exactly like I'd have been until recently. A lifetime ago.

The corridors were deserted. All the civilians were confined to their quarters, and we guessed the soldiers were busy evicting the 'crazies', as Spencer had called them. That and searching for a hunched, hairy murderer.

The lab door had been propped back into its frame. But with the lock and hinge broken it was easy enough to force it open. Inside, the place was a mess – papers across the floor, equipment broken, glassware smashed ... One of the operating tables had toppled over. I felt a moment of anger and fear as I looked at it, remembering what had so nearly happened here to me. And Anna.

'What now?' I wondered. 'Smash everything that's still intact?'

'Or just switch it off.' Anna was pulling plugs from wall sockets and disconnecting any cables and wires she could find. I started on the other side of the room, doing the same. I hadn't really been aware of the background hum of it all until its died away.

'Will that be enough, do you think?' I asked.

For good measure, I pushed over the metal archway. Cables sparked and snapped as it crashed to the floor. Anna was grinning, and so was I – it was immensely satisfying to see the thing collapse.

Our smiles faded as a slow hand-clapping came from just behind us. We turned to find Midnight standing there, watching us in amusement.

'Very enterprising,' he said. 'Though I doubt that Dr Kustler will be so impressed.' Several skitters edged towards us, flexing their clawed talons and chittering with eager anticipation. 'Which reminds me,' Midnight went on, 'we have some unfinished business. Are you still undecided?' he asked.

'I never was. I've come to my decision,' I told him defiantly.

Midnight sighed and made a point of inspecting

his fingernails. 'How sad. But never mind. You've come to your decision and now you'll have to live with it.'

Anna and I backed away as the skitters tensed, ready to pounce. Leathery wings unfolded and lazily beat the air.

'Or rather,' Midnight said, 'you've come to your decision and now you'll have to *die* with it.' He snapped his fingers and unleashed the skitters.

With Midnight there, I didn't think there was any point trying my time dial. Even if wrecking Kustler's equipment had made a difference, Midnight would stop us playing with time.

So I grabbed Anna and shoved her out of the way of the skitters. She stumbled, but didn't fall. Then we were both running, skitters at our heels – snapping and clawing. Midnight was blocking our way to either of the doors, so we ran for the only other exit – the passageway past the glassed-in observation cells.

We leaped through the broken window into the room where old Jeff had been kept. We'd done this before.

'Déjà vu,' I gasped at Anna.

113

'Knew you'd say that,' she told me, wrenching open the door and racing out the other side.

I slammed the door behind me as we headed back towards the office area. I glanced behind me as I ran – in time to see the metal door sag, buckle and rust away as if it was suddenly a thousand years old. The skitters piled through, clawing and scratching at each other in their excitement and haste.

'We need to get far enough away from Midnight,' Anna said as we ran. She paused to catch her breath back before she finished the thought. 'Far enough away for our time dials to work.'

'We hope,' I said.

Out of the office and down another corridor – into the older section of the former school. Back towards the dormitories.

'You think wrecking the equipment helped?' I asked.

'Only one way to find out.'

'Think we've got far enough?'

Anna half smiled. '*Still* only one way to find out.'

We both stopped at the bottom of a staircase.

Anna held the post at the bottom of the banisters as she gasped for breath. I was doubled over, hands on knees. 'Forwards or back?' I asked between gasps.

Before she could answer, the first of the skitters hurtled round the corner of the corridor and flew at us. I could feel the draught from its wings as they hammered at the air, propelling it forwards. Another skitter appeared behind the first.

And another behind that.

'Forwards,' Anna yelled.

We both slapped at the black dials on our wrists. Sharp claws slashed the air right in front of my face.

🕐 FRIDAY 19TH MARCH 2021

There was hardly any difference. Except that suddenly the skitters were gone. But apart from that, nothing much to show we'd travelled forward twenty-four hours. The light dimmed, then reappeared. But I could feel it. Our time dials worked again.

'We can't escape Midnight forever,' Anna

pointed out. 'But it should give us some breathing space.'

I was still gasping. 'Oh, good. Need that.' I straightened up and took another deep breath. 'So, are we done here, do you think? We've destroyed the time experiments.'

'What if Dr Kustler mends his equipment and keeps going?'

'Fair point,' I conceded.

'And we don't really know why Midnight is here. I don't believe that stuff about vital components. He doesn't need this coordinator thing at all.'

'Yeah, OK.'

'And there's the murders – what's going on there?'

'All right, a few loose ends, then.' We started up the stairs, heading towards the dormitories. 'So, where should we start, do you reckon?' I asked.

We'd just reached the first landing. There was a door facing the top of the stairs. I'd noticed it before, but never looked inside. Now it was cordoned off with strips of yellow and black tape. And there was a soldier standing guard outside.

'Where do you think we should start?' Anna said.

The soldier watched us suspiciously. We smiled back and carried on up to the next landing.

'He's probably wondering where we've been for the last twenty-four hours,' Anna said.

'I'm wondering what's behind that door he's guarding.'

'And why it's been taped off,' Anna agreed.

'Like a crime scene.'

It had been a workroom. There was a wooden table with a sewing machine on it. An ironing board was propped up against the wall. A chest of small drawers stood beside the table. I pulled open a few drawers and peered inside – buttons, thread, safety pins.

'They must have mended the kids' clothes in here,' I said. 'You know, sewing buttons back on shirts and doing the ironing and stuff.'

Anna looked at me like I was Sherlock Holmes. Well, that's not true actually. She looked at me like she was Sherlock Holmes and I was Police Constable Dimwitty of Scotland Yard's Obvious Observations Unit. 'You think?' she said.

We'd stopped time so we could look inside the room. The guard was frozen outside. The door hadn't been locked and we'd ducked under the tape and closed the door behind us.

'So why is this room guarded?' I wondered. 'What happened in here?'

Anna sighed and pointed at the floor. 'Any more deductions?'

The floor was bare wooden boards, dusty and uneven. But chalked across them in the middle of the room was the rough outline of a body. Just like they do on TV. Only not as neat. It looked as if it had been done in a hurry by someone who knew they were probably wasting their time.

'Another murder,' I said. 'And in the last twenty-four hours or we'd have known.'

'Seems like it,' Anna agreed.

I knelt down by the outline and examined it. 'They actually use chalk,' I said. 'I'd have thought it was paint or something, or sticky tape.'

'This was a school,' Anna said. 'There's probably no shortage of chalk.'

I thought of mentioning that education might have moved on from the 1950s and they'd have white boards and felt-tip markers now. But a nasty thought had occurred to me. 'You don't suppose those skitters that were chasing us . . .'

'What?' Anna said. 'You think they lost us so they found some other victim and killed them?'

'Maybe.'

'They don't work like that,' she said. But she didn't sound as confident as I'd have liked. 'Not usually. Who knows?' She was getting exasperated now. 'You tell me.'

'OK.' I forced a grin. 'Let's take this room back twenty-four hours, then wind through and see what did happen in here.'

Anna grinned too. 'Good idea. So, you're not just a pretty face, then.'

'Less of the "pretty" if you don't mind.' I wondered if Anna knew how pretty *she* was. I didn't ask.

We stood by the wall, close to the door, and rewound to the previous day. The room was empty and the door was shut. It looked very much the same. Except without the chalked outline on the floor.

'We need to go forward a bit,' Anna said.

She let me do it. She liked to say I was getting better at these things than she was, but maybe she actually thought I needed the practice. Like at the bottom of the stairs when we escaped from the skitters, it was difficult to see any difference. The quality of the light changed, but what illumination there was came through the dust and grime that coated the window in a grubby film.

Then, abruptly, there was someone in the room.

'Stop. Go back.'

I did. Reality paused for a moment as time changed direction – long enough for us to see that the person who had come into the room was Mrs Dorril.

'I hope . . .' I began.

I hoped it wasn't Mrs Dorril who was destined to be outlined in chalk on the floor. She did at least seem to care about the children she was keeping safe for Kustler's unpleasant experiments. It was as if neither she nor Alford approved of what was going on. Though they hadn't put a stop to it.

Anna did not seem to have heard me. She was watching time roll backwards and Mrs Dorril walk backwards out of the room. The door closed.

'Right, let it run from there.'

The door opened again – although it was actually for the first time – and Mrs Dorril came into the room. She looked round, as if expecting to find someone else there.

'Hello?' she called softly, though it was obvious the room was empty.

Well, I suppose we were there, only we weren't really. Not so Mrs Dorril could tell. There was a bubble in the middle of the room, extending to the door and window, a bubble in which time had rolled back to replay events from the past, from *our* past. Anna and I were standing outside that bubble, looking into it. Mrs Dorril couldn't see us. She'd just see the wall as it was in her own time. Perhaps a goldfish sees the glass side of its bowl and not the children looking in at it.

Mrs Dorril seemed slightly nervous. Not all-out about-to-be-murdered nervous. Just a bit on edge. She walked slowly round the room. Then she turned and paced back the other way. She checked her watch. Walked, checked her watch again. Then she turned and stared right at us.

'Er, she can't see us, can she?' I asked.

'Of course not.'

'Just checking.'

So was Mrs Dorril. Checking her watch for a third time. As she did so, the door swung slowly open. It didn't open fully, and we were standing so the door blocked our view on to the landing outside as it opened into the room.

But whoever was there, Mrs Dorril sighed with relief. 'I was about to give up,' she said. 'We really do need to talk. This can't go on – the children. We just can't, not any more.' She looked round nervously. 'Though why you wanted to meet and discuss it here . . .'

She hesitated, frowning.

Though we couldn't see who was standing just outside the door, their shadow was falling into the room. Long and distorted. Whoever it was took a step forwards and the shadow moved with them. It seemed to shift and distort. It widened and changed, like your reflection when you walk through a fairground hall of mirrors.

Mrs Dorril took a step backwards. 'Are you OK?' Her frown was deepening. 'What's the matter? Oh my –' Words seemed to fail her and she took another step backwards, hand pressed to her mouth as if to stop herself saying anything more.

The figure stepped into the room. Hunched and misshapen. Its deep-set eyes seemed to glow red in the dim light of the room. Its broad body was covered with thick dark hair, so dense it was almost like fur. The long arms that swung by the creature's side ended in massive paws. Massive paws that reached out for Mrs Dorril as she shrank away, whimpering.

'No – please, no . . .'

Then the long, thick fingers closed on her throat.

Anna turned away and pressed her face into my shoulder, unable to look. I turned away too. We knew how it would end. I didn't need – didn't *want* – to see it. Just the sounds were bad enough – coughing, whimpering, sighing. The crunch of bone, and grunts of effort as the thing throttled the life from Mrs Dorril and let her body slump to the ground at its feet. I recognised the shape of the body from the chalk outline that wasn't there yet.

'What is it?' Anna sobbed into my shoulder. 'What is that thing?'

'Don't know,' I managed to say. My throat was so dry it was an effort to speak.

I forced myself to look. Anna was slowly turning as well.

The ape-like creature was standing over the body. It sniffed, as if catching the scent of another victim, and looked round. It stared into each corner of the room, as if sensing it was being watched. The red eyes flicked from one shadow to another, from dusty corner to half-open door.

They came to rest at last – staring at us.

'Sure it can't see us?' I said. I meant it as a joke. But my voice was husky and shaking.

'Not unless it exists somehow outside time,' Anna said. She sounded as anxious as I did.

'That's all right, then,' I said, trying to sound more at ease.

The creature gave a satisfied grunt, as if assured that it was alone and unobserved. But the grunt became a ferocious roar of triumph. The air in front of us seemed to split open, like someone had pulled back a sheet of almost clear plastic to reveal the true depth and colour and clarity of the scene beyond.

And the creature leaped through time – right at us.

Anna gave a shriek of both surprise and fear. Again, I pushed her out of the way of some serious claws. This time, she did fall. The creature turned, looming over her. I launched myself at it, trying to knock the thing away as it snarled and reached down at Anna.

I might as well have run at a wall. The creature was solid and I staggered back, the wind knocked out of me. The creature's claws slashed down towards Anna's terrified face.

Then the door opened. Time had started again when the monster came through from the past. Somehow its arrival had affected things and the guard outside the door had heard Anna's scream. He stared at the creature, his mouth open in astonishment. He fumbled with the catch on his holster, struggling to draw his handgun.

The massive creature gave a snarl of rage and leaped over Anna's body. The guard, his gun ready now, aimed.

But too late – the creature hammered into the man, sending him flying backwards, out of the room and across the landing. He slammed into the banister rail at the top of the stairs and sagged to the floor. His gun bounced down the staircase.

I pulled Anna to her feet and we ran from the room. The monster was reaching down for the soldier. The man's eyes were wide, terrified. He screamed.

We were already running, sprinting through the nearest door, into the boys' dormitory. Running full tilt past the curtained cubicles.

'What is it?' I gasped.

'You ask,' Anna told me.

But I was worrying about something else. We'd not had any choice about where to run. The problem now was, the stairs were the only way out of the dormitory. And the creature – whatever it was – stood between us and the way out. We might have evaded it for now, but it had us trapped. I felt Anna hesitate slightly as we ran – she knew it too.

Behind us, the soldier had stopped screaming. I risked a look back, over my shoulder. The creature was straightening up, beginning to turn – so it was now or never. I dragged Anna sideways, into one of the cubicles, fighting past the curtain.

Anna looked at me, opening her hands to silently demand, 'Now what?'

'Out of the window?' I suggested.

'Very funny. We're four floors up.'

The sound of the creature's heavy footsteps was like the thumping of my heart. The steps hesitated. Like it was looking round. Could it see us through the curtain?

We both realised at the same moment – it could see us *under* the curtain, which stopped fifteen centimetres above the bare wooden floor. Anna stepped up on to the bed and I followed, afraid it would creak under the weight and give us away. We struggled to keep absolutely still.

The noise we heard then made us both grab the other and hold tight in an embrace that would otherwise have been really embarrassing. But we had heard the sudden rapid scrape of metal curtain rings across metal pole. The creature had drawn back the curtain of one of the nearby cubicles.

Then another, closer to us. Followed almost at once by a third – closer still.

When it threw back the curtain on our cubicle – which we both knew it would – the creature would find us. And there was nowhere to go.

Another curtain opened – almost next to us. Getting closer . . . Then I had an idea – a desperate idea, but it might just work. The walls between the cubicles were just wooden partitions. They were about two metres high. But the ceiling was another metre above that. If we timed it right . . .

I don't think Anna had any notion what I was trying to tell her as I pulled away and pointed, gestured, mouthed at her. Another curtain – perhaps two cubicles away on the other side of the dormitory. I risked a whisper, quiet as I could, right in her ear.

'You're mad!' she mouthed back at me.

I couldn't really disagree. But I couldn't think of anything else to do. If we stayed put, we'd be monster fodder.

I saw the shadows on the ceiling ripple as the curtain of the next cubicle to ours was ripped away. Rings bounced on the rail as the material tore.

'Now!' I mouthed urgently at Anna.

Our curtain twitched, distorted as a huge paw grabbed it from the other side.

We were up on the top of the cubicle partition, pivoting on our stomachs. Like getting out of a swimming pool, except then we were falling down the other side. I heard the curtain rip open. We both landed on the bed in the next cubicle together.

I hadn't thought of the noise it would make. The creak of the bedsprings. A split second of exchanged, frightened looks. Then Anna and I ran.

Out of the cubicle, as the creature turned towards us. But we were the right side of it now – heading for the stairs and a way out. Running. Hand in hand. Almost laughing with relief. But not out of danger yet, as we both heard the thump of its feet starting after us.

A shadow appeared at the end of the dormitory. A figure stepping into the light from the top of the stairs. A dark silhouette, legs slightly apart, hands raised.

Aiming a gun. Alford, standing braced, aiming a handgun right at us. Anna and I skidded to a halt. The creature gave a roar of triumph and leaped at us.

Alford couldn't miss at that range. The barrel of the gun seemed to grow larger, blacker, before exploding into light. Two shots in rapid succession. Right at me and Anna.

Or rather, right between us. I turned in time to see the creature lifted off its feet and hurled back down the dormitory. It skidded along the floor as it landed, roaring in pain.

'Is it dead?' Anna wondered aloud.

'Should be,' Alford told her.

But the creature was already hauling itself to its feet.

'Should be, but isn't,' I yelled. 'Come on!'

'I spend my life running,' Anna grumbled. But there wasn't time for me to agree or sympathise.

The soldier's body was blocking the top of the stairs down, so we went up. Alford pushing us ahead of him. The creature's ragged breath receded behind us and it seemed the bullets had at least slowed it down even if they hadn't stopped it.

'Can we get out up here?' I asked as we reached the next landing.

'Nope,' Alford replied.

'Oh, great,' Anna said.

We ran down the girls' dormitory and were soon in another cubicle.

'So, do we just hope it gives up on us, or crawls away to die?' I said.

'We call in the troops,' Alford said. He had his radio out and was already thumbing the call button.

'What is that animal?' Anna demanded as Alford gave orders into the radio. 'I've never seen anything like it.'

'I have.' It was Alford who answered, putting his radio away. 'Years ago. When I was in the Secret Service. Not like that exactly. But savage, inexplicable. Out of nowhere.'

Anna and I were staring at him – what could he mean?

'It's happening again. A monster from nowhere. Nothing like the same, but a monster,' Alford went on. 'It was a monster that killed the president. When you've seen that happen, nothing surprises you any more.'

Anna and I looked at each other, wide-eyed. Then back at Alford.

'What?' Anna said. 'What are you talking about?'

'The president fell – an accident,' I said at the same time. But I was remembering the dog – or whatever it was. The animal on the roof.

'That's the official story.' Alford clicked the magazine out of the handle of his gun and checked how many bullets he had left. Then he clicked it back into place. 'Tragic accident. President Carlton fell to his death from a high-rise. Caught by a freak crosswind as he waited for his helicopter – Marine One – to pick him up.' Alford looked at us grimly. 'That's what all this is about – this place. That's what Kustler is so desperate to prevent. But it wasn't an accident.' He had the gun up, ready. 'It was an assassination.'

'Why don't people know all about this?' I remembered what Anna had said about the rumours. 'Why cover it up?'

'Why do you think? You've seen what's

happened to the country. The paranoia, retrench-
ment. Isolationism. People feeling they're under
attack – and that was when it was reported as
an accident. Imagine if they thought someone
deliberately killed their president? Who's next
on the list? What now? Who can we trust? Are
we at war? If so, with whom?'

'We get the idea,' Anna said.

I nodded. 'But – monsters? What's that all
about?'

'You tell me. Maybe something's trying to stop
Kustler's work. Maybe it's all connected . . .' He
sighed. 'Listen to me, I'm paranoid – I've thought
of nothing else since it happened except why I
didn't save the president.'

Alford looked out from the cubicle, gun at
the ready. There didn't seem to be any sign of the
creature. Not yet. But then it could afford to
take its time. Anna was desperately trying to get
her time dial to work. Good idea, I thought –
if nothing else we could go and see what really
happened on that roof all those years ago . . .

The sound came from behind us and we all
jumped, visibly. Alford swung round immediately, gun levelled, finger tightening on the trigger.

It was Florence, stepping out from a cubicle further down the dormitory. 'I heard you talking. I was taking a rest.' She stared at the gun and swallowed.

But Alford was already breathing a sigh of relief and turning to check the other way, back towards the stairs.

'What are you talking about?' Florence asked again. 'You said something about President Carlton being assassinated.'

'Yeah,' I told her. 'By a monster. Now there's another monster after us.'

'This one is different,' Alford said, without looking round. 'It seems more ... I dunno – human. Like an ape. The thing that got Carlton was ... like a big rabid dog or a wolf or something.' He shook his head. 'I never want to see anything like that again as long as I live.' He turned to smile reassuringly at us. 'And don't worry – that's for a long while yet.'

'You sure about that?' Anna asked quietly.

At the other end of the dormitory, the shadows were deepening, as something large and hairy and furious leaped up on to the landing and turned towards us.

· CHAPTER ELEVEN ·

We backed slowly away as the monstrous creature lumbered down the dormitory towards us. Alford's bullets didn't seem to have slowed it down much. I doubted that shooting it again would do anything to help. Probably just make it angry. Since Alford wasn't blazing away at the thing with his gun, I guessed he thought the same.

'What is that?' Florence said in a harsh whisper. She started walking towards it, fascinated and horrified at the same time.

I grabbed her arm and gently pulled her back. 'You don't want to know. In fact, none of us knows.' It was something to do with time itself – to do with the experiments, I was sure. But what?

136

It had come through time at me and Anna.

'Is it something to do with Midnight?' I asked Anna. 'Not a skitter, but some other pet of his?'

She shook her head. 'Maybe. I don't know.'

'Midnight?' Alford said. 'You mean Mr Knight?'

'Yes. He's not what he seems,' Anna told him.

Alford gave a grunt of amusement, though his eyes were still fixed on the approaching creature. 'He seems to me like a nasty piece of work.'

'OK,' I said. 'Maybe he is what he seems, then.'

'Doesn't help us now, though,' Anna pointed out.

Florence made a short high-pitched noise that might have been agreement, or frustration, or fright. Probably fright. I could feel my whole body shaking as I took another step backwards. It was an effort to stop my legs wobbling away from under me.

The creature paused in front of us, swaying from side to side on its powerful, hairy legs. It reminded me of a gorilla I'd seen at the zoo – long arms hanging lazily by its side, but ready to tear apart anyone who annoyed it. Smelled the same too – sort of musky and sweaty and stale. Its eyes were points of red in the dark face, shadowed by heavy brows. But Alford was right, there was something 'human' about it. Something in the face, the expression. The really weird thing was, it reminded me of someone . . .

As the creature swayed, gathering itself ready to attack, there was more movement at the top of the stairs. Behind the creature, several soldiers were moving into position. One of them was gesturing to another two, pointing, waving, positioning them ready to attack. I hoped their guns would have more effect than Alford's.

Then suddenly the creature was moving. It launched itself towards us. Florence screamed. Alford yelled at the soldiers. Anna grabbed me. The crack of bullets echoed round the room.

The shots caught the creature in the back, driving it forwards – towards us. We scattered. Only Alford stood his ground, shooting back. Then he dived aside as the creature came at him. He was lucky to avoid being shot by his own men.

But the creature was still between us and the stairs – between us and any chance of escape. Worse still, it seemed angered rather than injured. I could see the holes torn in the matted fur that covered its body where the bullets hit. But it ignored them, snarling with rage and turning to and fro as it looked for someone to rip to shreds.

The soldiers were moving slowly along the dormitory, still firing. One of them was out of ammunition. He dropped the magazine out of his gun with practised ease and slammed another one in. Fired again.

Again with little effect.

Florence gave a shriek of fright and ran for it – hoping to get past the beast's thrashing arms. But she didn't stand a chance. One of the soldiers yelled for them to stop firing – otherwise she'd have been shot to pieces before she reached the monster.

As it was, she was running right at it, screaming and waving her arms, tears streaking down her face. It swayed, waiting, as events seemed to play out in slow motion. Anna and I could do nothing. Anna turned away.

'No – look!' I told her.

She stared at me like I was Mr Sick-brain. But I wasn't being nasty. Something was happening. A blur of motion. The air shimmering between the soldiers as something raced towards the creature from behind as it reached for Florence. Something no one could see, except me and Anna.

A skitter.

And then another. Four of them – scrabbling and skidding across the wooden floor. Grabbing at the monster. It was so huge they had to jump as they grabbed at its legs. A fifth skitter flew at its back, great leathery wings flapping madly as it tried to hold on and pull the creature away from Florence.

Alford and the soldiers were watching in amazement as the creature swayed on its feet, desperately flailing to keep its balance. They couldn't see the skitters, so they must have thought the gunfire had finally got to it. Florence ran past and kept going. She disappeared past the tall, thin figure that was striding into the dormitory. The tall, thin figure that paused only to touch the brim of his hat in greeting before continuing his purposeful walk down the dormitory. Midnight was back in his usual hat and cane get-up, dark cloak swirling round him as he strode towards the creature.

He reached it as the skitters succeeded in bringing it down. Like hounds attacking a bear, they kept at it until the creature buckled and fell. Still it roared and thrashed out. It caught one of the skitters, sending it flying backwards into a cubicle with a wail of surprise. A moment later it appeared like a sheepish gargoyle peering out from behind the curtain as its fellows fought and nipped and clawed and bit.

The soldiers were grouped round the flailing creature, guns aimed, oblivious to the skitters that were all over it. The commander glanced up at Alford for the order to shoot.

But before Alford could make his decision, Midnight stepped between two of the soldiers and stood over the creature. It looked up at him for a moment, as if sensing his power.

Then Midnight slammed his cane down, the silver top hammering into the creature's head. The red of its eyes disappeared into the darkness of its fur and it fell back. Silent and still.

'Mind telling us what's going on, sir?' one of the soldiers asked Alford.

'I wish I knew,' he said. 'This got something to do with you, Mr Knight?' He was looking at

Midnight suspiciously. 'And what's with the fancy dress?'

'It's just crazy,' one of the other soldiers said.

'It's about to get a whole lot weirder,' Midnight told him, in that fake American accent of his. 'Take a look.' He pointed at the unconscious body of the monster, tapping it on the side with his cane.

I could see there was something odd about it. The whole thing was shimmering, like when you almost, but not quite, see a skitter. But the skitters were with Midnight now, playing in and out of his cape and staying close to their master. One of them bared its teeth at me and snarled. I ignored it.

I looked back at the creature. It was a shimmering blur, its shape lost in the misty swirl of the air. It seemed to be shrinking, changing . . . The dark hair faded to pale skin. The heavy brow receded and human features began to emerge – proper human features. I'd thought I recognised the face – some semblance of someone I knew.

Now I could see why. Because lying on the dormitory floor in front of us was not an aggressive, hairy monster. It was a man. It was Dr Kustler.

He opened his eyes and blinked, as surprised to see us as we were to see him. 'What's going on here?' he demanded. Then he realised he was lying naked on the floor.

Midnight unclipped his cloak and draped it over Kustler.

'I think you owe us an explanation,' Alford said, his voice quiet but with a dangerous edge to it. 'A whole load of explanations.'

Kustler struggled to his feet, pulling the cloak round him. 'I don't ... What's happening?' To say he was confused is to put it pretty mildly.

'The time experiments,' Anna said. 'Something's gone wrong with them, hasn't it?' She was looking at me, but it was Midnight who answered.

'Evolution, but in reverse.' He was examining Kustler, looking carefully at the man's face and into his eyes, inspecting the roots of his hair. 'You experimented on yourself, didn't you? When you thought you had it working. Before you started on the children. But there was a problem, wasn't there? That's why you needed to experiment on others – on people you thought wouldn't be missed if anything else went wrong.'

'Which it did,' Anna said.

'You mean, he went through the archway?' I said. 'But then why isn't he old like Jeff?'

'Or a baby?' Anna said. 'That's what the experiments do, isn't it? You can't travel backwards and forwards in time. Instead, time travels backwards or forwards for you. You get younger or you get older, but you don't move through time.'

'Not without a synchronisation coordinator,' Midnight said. 'And the effect of that first experiment was so much more extreme. Temporary, or so you thought, but extreme. You went back so far – time regressed into the distant past. You evolved backwards into what Man used to be.'

Kustler looked away, as if he was embarrassed. 'It only lasted a few seconds. That first time,' he said quietly. 'I thought it was over. And it wasn't anything like so extreme. I was almost human. But it keeps coming back.' He put his hand over his face. 'It keeps coming back. Every time for longer, every time more of a monster. I can't stop

144

it.' He looked at us again, face contorted with fear and anger. 'Don't you understand? I can't stop it.'

'I can,' Midnight said. 'Let's get him to the lab.'

I guess because no one had a better idea, and it seemed that Midnight knew all about it, Alford agreed.

'I don't trust Midnight,' I said to Anna as we followed the soldiers, Alford and Kustler. I watched Midnight swinging his cane confidently as he led the way.

'Neither do I,' Anna said. 'But unless you have another suggestion . . .'

'I guess they can't just shoot him,' I said.

'Midnight or Kustler?'

'Well, either,' I said. 'Or maybe both. But I really meant Kustler.'

'I guess they can't,' Anna agreed. 'Poor man. He was desperate to go back in time and instead time went back *for* him.'

'They can't carry on after this, can they?' I wondered.

'Then why are we going to the lab?' Anna said.

'And what's Midnight up to?' I sighed. 'I suppose this means we can't leave just yet, then.'

'But I've a feeling it won't be long. Whatever is really going on here, it's coming to the end.'

She was right. I could feel it – a sense of foreboding. A sense that even as they became clearer, things were becoming more dangerous. And there was nothing we could do about it.

The old man was blinking in surprise. His watery grey eyes looked tired rather than frightened as two soldiers helped him into the room.

'Hello, Jeff,' I said. He looked at me, but his expression didn't change. I couldn't tell if he was he blaming me, thanking me or just totally confused.

Florence had joined us again and brought Kate and Spencer with her. They stood at the back of the laboratory watching.

'That really Jeff?' Kate asked. 'You're kidding, right?'

'No, we're not,' Anna said.

Midnight ignored the interruption. He was

147

working on the equipment. The bits and pieces that Anna and I had pulled apart were reconnected, and he was adding what looked like a glass ball into the tangle of wires and circuits attached to the archway, which was upright again if a little skewed. When he had finished, it hung there like a Christmas tree bauble.

Dr Kustler sat with his head in his hands on one of the chairs. He was wearing a white lab coat instead of Midnight's cloak. But his bare legs and feet stuck out from beneath. 'It won't work,' he said without looking up. 'I've tried. Older or younger, but once they've been through it doesn't affect them again.' He looked up at us, eyes bloodshot and face pale. 'You think I haven't tried? I put them back through – all of them. Reversed the settings, hoped and prayed they'd change back. Me too, of course.'

Midnight stepped aside to admire his work. 'Ah,' he said, 'but you didn't have a synchronisation coordinator.'

'That glass thing?' I asked.

Midnight nodded. 'You were so nearly there,' he told Kustler. 'You were on the right track. Another day or two and you'd have worked it out. A shame to have to intervene, but I sense that things have gone far enough.'

'You're telling me,' I muttered.

'So what's that do, then?' Spencer asked. He cringed away as Midnight turned towards him. 'Er, if you don't mind me asking, sir?'

'Let's see, shall we?' Midnight said. He set the controls on a nearby console and then nodded to the two soldiers holding Jeff. 'You can send him through now.'

But Jeff was shaking his head. 'I ain't going through that thing.' His voice was dry and cracked. 'No way. Never again.'

'It's for your own good,' Midnight assured him.

'I bet,' Anna said. 'You can't make him go through.'

Midnight spared her a glance, no more. 'Make him go through,' he told the soldiers. 'But keep clear yourselves.' Like they needed telling.

The soldiers gave Jeff a rough push and he stumbled through the archway, crying out in his brittle, old man's voice. The weak cry became a strong shout of defiance. The figure in the arch seemed to blur and change – to straighten up and fill out. His stumble became more controlled and he regained some of his balance. And a young man – the kid we'd met on the bus all that time ago – stumbled out of the other side of the archway.

'Hey ...' Jeff said. He stared at his hands – smooth and young now, not old and wrinkled. 'What did ...' He looked up, a series of expressions working their way across his face as he went through fear, confusion, astonishment and finally delight. 'What d'yer know?' he finally said. 'I'm ... back.'

His expression changed again as Kate ran across the room and hugged him tight.

'Oh, gross! Do me a favour,' Florence said, and turned away.

There were another half-dozen to go through the arch – some old, a toddler who could just about walk through on his own and the baby. They rolled the baby through on a small lab trolley – it gurgled with delight, thinking this was a game.

But the gurgle became a cry of surprise as Midnight draped his cloak over the girl that emerged on the other side.

'What are you all staring at?' she demanded, getting carefully to her feet as the trolley tipped and skidded beneath her.

'Hi, Chrissy,' Florence said.

The girl glared back. 'Whatever.'

The kids went off to the common room. Florence, Spencer and Kate wanted to know all about it, while the others – the ones who had just 'come back', as Jeff had put it – were mostly rather less talkative. In shock, probably.

Which left me and Anna with Midnight, 'General' Alford, a couple of soldiers and Kustler.

Kustler seemed a changed man. Not changed like turned into a reverse-evolutionary creature of death, no – changed as in interested and enthusiastic. Wanting to know all about the synchronisation coordinator that Midnight had wired into his experiments.

'But that's exactly what I've been trying to achieve,' he said when Midnight deigned to explain a little.

'Well, you should have been quicker at it,' Midnight told him.

'Least everything's sorted now,' Alford said. 'The kids can go home, or back to where they came from, and no real harm done.'

Anna gave a snort of outraged amusement at that. Like a few murders was 'no harm'. But Alford ignored her.

'This place will be shut down,' he announced. 'Dismantled. Decommissioned.' He turned to the two soldiers standing by the equipment. 'Yes, gentlemen, we're going home too. It's time Senator Georgeson got this country sorted out. He's made a start, judging by the reaction to his speeches the other day. Now we can go help him finish it.'

Kustler leaped to his feet at this. 'But we don't need Georgeson.' He looked from Alford to Midnight, eyes shining with enthusiasm. 'Don't you see? Mr Knight's done it. With this synchronisation coordinator, I can do it.'

'Do what?' Alford asked.

I felt suddenly cold in the pit of my stomach as I realised. I felt Anna staring at me – she knew too.

'I can go back, like we always planned. That's why we set this place up and now we can do it.

I can do it. I can go back and save President Carlton.'

Alford took a step back in surprise. 'You could do that?'

Kustler nodded. 'I could. I can go back to the rooftop, warn the president – warn *you*. You failed him back then, and I know you've blamed yourself ever since. Blamed yourself for what happened and what you did, the decisions you made.' He reached out and took hold of Alford's hands. Maybe pleading, maybe reassuring. 'But I can make it all OK. I can sort it out. I can stop this country's fall into anarchy and chaos. We won't need Senator Georgeson.'

I could see Alford struggling to come to terms with this and decide what to do. He looked from Kustler to Midnight. He stared for a moment at the archway.

'You can really do it? You're sure?'

Kustler nodded.

Midnight watched them carefully, his face giving nothing away. Was this why he was here – to put everything right and back on track somehow? Or were events getting away from him? Did he want the president saved or not? I

153

looked at Anna and she shrugged. It was up to Alford.

'No,' Alford said.

Kustler blinked. 'I'm sorry?'

'No. You get yourself sorted out. Then this place is being taken apart.'

'But – you don't understand!' Kustler grabbed him again, but Alford shook him off.

'I understand all too well. I made decisions, choices. I did what I could, what I thought was for the best. Could I have saved Carlton if I'd acted differently? I don't know. But you're right about one thing – I blame myself. I blame myself every single minute of every single day. For Carlton and for the deaths here too. But the past is the past. Maybe we can change it, but we shouldn't.'

'How can you say that?' Kustler demanded. 'Look at what's happening to this country.'

'It isn't happening because of Carlton's death. OK, he held us together and maybe Georgeson will pull us back together. But our history and our future depend on the decisions that all of us take. And I've just taken mine. You set the controls to sort you out and get you fixed and cured

154

and OK. Then after you step through that archway, this ends. Got it?'

I thought Kustler was going to argue back. But after a moment he just nodded and stepped away. 'All right,' he said quietly, head down, obviously disappointed. He went over to the controls and he and Midnight changed some settings.

'That should do it,' Midnight said.

Kustler nodded. 'Should indeed.' He smiled at Midnight.

And Midnight smiled back.

There was something about that smile. Something that told me it was all wrong.

Anna sensed it too. She shouted, 'No – stop him!'

That was all the confirmation I needed. I ran.

Kustler was already stepping through the archway. I grabbed at him and caught hold of the lab coat, pulling him back. But the coat came away in my hands as he stumbled through the archway. I was off balance too. Falling – trying to stay upright. Over-correcting. Falling after Kustler through the archway.

In front of me I could see Kustler's body shimmering and changing. The background was changing too. Instead of the laboratory, I could see the blue sky and I could hear the thump of a helicopter's rotor blades ... Kustler was transforming again, but it was more extreme this time, just as he'd described. Another trip through the archway seemed to have exaggerated the process. For a moment he was a hunched, muscular, ape-like figure covered in matted black fur. But then he pitched forwards, his arms becoming forelegs, his face stretching into a wolf-like snout. A fierce, angry nightmare of a creature. It snarled with rage and anger.

From behind me I heard Anna shouting, Midnight laughing.

And Alford exclaiming in shocked disbelief, 'That's it. That's what I saw. That's what killed the president!'

CHAPTER THIRTEEN

🕐 **TUESDAY 3RD MAY 2016**

I couldn't stop time, or slow it or change it at all. The creature that Kustler had become was still somehow blocking my time dial. I couldn't do it without the dial either – maybe it was blocking that too, or perhaps I just couldn't, not then. It comes and goes, the power . . .

I'd arrived on the top of the Judson Building just behind the creature. We were in the shadow of the little hut-like structure where the staircase emerged onto the roof. The president was striding out towards the arriving helicopter, security staff and aides with him. The helicopter was just touching down, its wheels springing under its weight but its rotors were still spinning

157

fast and noisy. Too noisy for me to shout a warning – I know, I tried. My voice was lost.

Which was just as well. It was probably too late, and with what was about to happen the Secret Service would probably have shot me.

The creature was shouting too – yelling in a low, guttural, wordless voice. I could just hear it, but no one else was close enough. Frustrated, it broke into a shambling run, as if unused to having four legs.

I was about to run after it when a hand closed on my shoulder. I whirled round – astonished and afraid. But it was Anna.

'You came through after me,' I said in surprise.

Her hair was blowing round her face in the wind from the helicopter's rotors.

'Obviously.'

'You didn't have to do that.'

'I couldn't leave you on your own with that thing.'

'We're too late,' I yelled to her, turning back to see what was happening.

'I know,' Anna shouted in my ear. 'We were meant to be. We were always too late, right from when we arrived. This has already happened.

Kustler was never meant to stop it. He *is* it.'

'And that's why Midnight was there,' I realised with sudden horror. 'Not to change things for once, but to make sure they happened as he wanted, as they have to.'

The creature cut across the roof, heading straight for the president. Maybe he wanted to warn him, help him. Or maybe there was so little of Kustler left inside it that the thing was acting on pure instinct.

The Secret Service men saw it. Shouted. Their voices, like mine, were lost in the sound of the helicopter and their mouths moved urgently but silently. I could see the creature's fur rippling in the wind. And Carlton's sudden terror as he saw it heading right for him, jaws snapping as it tried to speak. The president ran.

More shouts. Weapons coming up. The roar of the helicopter. The creature racing after the president. Arriving at the edge of the roof. The Secret Service agent in charge talking urgently into his lapel microphone – Alford, younger and thinner and with more hair. But definitely Alford.

'They can't shoot or they might hit the president,' I realised.

The creature reared up, stretched out a paw —
trying to explain, to help. Or so I imagined.

And the president hurled himself backwards in
terror, away from the monster that was clawing
at him. And over the edge — off the top of the
building.

Immediately the gunshots rang out — a deadly
drumbeat, driving the creature back and over
the edge, after the president. As the bullets hit,
the creature's mouth was open in surprise, fear,
regret . . . And as it fell it changed.

A dead man followed the president, falling to
oblivion.

🕐 SATURDAY 20TH MARCH 2021

They were dismantling the laboratory. Men in
overalls and soldiers. Frozen. And of course
there was no sign of Midnight. He was long
gone.

Anna and I stood in the middle of the process
and looked round. The archway was already
gone. The wires and equipment that had been
attached to it were hanging loose, ready to be

disconnected. Several of the control consoles were also gone. Another was in pieces. The floor was a beach of broken glass. Alford stood at the side of the room, arms folded, watching with a determined expression fixed on his face.

'We should just let them get on with it,' Anna said. 'Job done.'

'Time experiments over. And the damage had already been done.'

'If it was damage. We don't know what Midnight was up to or what would have happened if . . .' Anna shrugged.

But I knew what she meant – if we'd never come here. If we'd never got involved. For once Midnight had been keeping time in its tracks, not disrupting it. Or maybe he was making sure that some disruption he had already caused didn't get changed.

'It'll sort itself out,' I said. 'We can check in the library and see what happened after this, but, like Alford there said, Senator Georgeson is well on the way to dealing with things.'

'I suppose . . .' Anna sighed. 'Nothing more we can do here anyway. Let's just leave them to it.

161

I guess we did what Senex wanted. We stopped the experiments. And whether we like it or not, history hasn't been changed, time hasn't been damaged.'

I lifted the mass of tangled cables and wires that had been removed from the archway. As I had expected, there in the middle of it was the small translucent sphere that Midnight had added – the synchronisation coordinator that somehow opened up time so that Kustler could be put into it rather than travelling through it. The way Midnight said he'd been able to put Norman Sellwood back into time after he'd been taken out of it – lost, like us.

'What are you doing?' Anna asked.

'Just making sure. Without this, it's useless. They can't put it back together. At least, not so it works. This is the one thing that shouldn't be here, because Midnight put it there.'

I pulled it free from its connections and slipped it into my pocket. I had no idea how it worked, or if it would ever work again. But I didn't want anyone else to have it. And maybe – just maybe – one day it would work for me . . .

'Time to be going,' I said.

'Already gone,' Anna replied as reality blurred around us. Her voice came to me through a swirl of colours. 'In fact, I was never here at all.'

CHAPTER FOURTEEN

🕐 **WEDNESDAY 25TH OCTOBER 1854**

The horses' hooves kicked up the dust like smoke. The sound was like thunder and the noise of the cannon from the end of the valley amplified and enhanced it.

Anna and I turned away as the first of the cavalry fell. Horses reared up. Riders went flying.

Senex shook his head and sighed. 'Magnificent folly.'

'You brought us here to see that?' Anna asked.

'Not at all,' the old man said. 'I had some business to attend to earlier. Making sure they got the right valley. Or rather, the wrong one.'

He did not elaborate but led us away from the sight of the carnage below. We sat together on a

164

rocky outcrop, the sunlight filtering through the drifting smoke and the air smelling of gunpowder.

'You did well,' Senex said. 'Not what you – or I – expected. But the experiments are at an end and whatever happened was meant to happen.'

'You sure?' I asked.

'Sure enough,' he said. 'The real danger was that Kustler's meddling with time would cause catastrophic problems – perhaps even rupture the universe. Who knows? Yes, you are making excellent progress. You are a good team. I know you are disappointed at how things turned out, but you did well. Really, you did.'

'Thank you,' Anna said. She smiled at me, and suddenly the death and disaster below us seemed miles and years away.

But there was something I needed to know. I turned to Senex. 'Midnight had something called a synchronisation coordinator,' I said.

'Did he now?' Senex's expression did not alter.

'Yes. He used it to get Kustler's time experiments to work – to send him back to kill President Carlton.'

Anna knew what I wanted to ask. 'Midnight

said it could put us back into time,' she said. 'Send us home.'

Senex steepled his fingers as he considered his answer. 'What Midnight says and what is true are often very different things,' he said at last. Which did not actually answer the question.

'You mean he was lying?' I asked.

'Midnight used his power to make the equipment work when and how he wanted it to. I have no doubt about that. But as to whether there is a particular component that was responsible, or if that component could be used for other purposes, as you suggest ...' Senex shook his head.

'But why would he lie?' I insisted.

Senex's voice hardened. 'Because that is what he does. Do not believe him. Midnight has his own agenda, his own reasons for doing things. If he told you this synchronisation coordinator could help you, then he had a reason to say it. And that reason would have precious little to do with the truth — you can believe me when I tell you that.'

But could I? 'I guess we'll have to,' I said quietly.

Senex nodded. He smiled sadly, then patted me on the shoulder as if I was a good and obedient and trusted dog. 'If such a device existed, I would happily examine it and see if there is any truth in what Midnight told you. But sadly, I assume it was destroyed when Alford dismantled the equipment.'

It wasn't quite a question, but he expected an answer. I looked at Anna. Her eyes met mine and she gave the very slightest shake of her head.

'Yes,' I said. 'It was destroyed. So we'll never know, will we?'

'*I* know,' Senex said. 'Trust me.'

And I really did want to trust him. Even though it would mean that he was right and there was no way back for Anna or me. The only problem was, I didn't. Midnight had no reason to lie. Senex, I was beginning to suspect, might have . . .

'Now, I'm sure you could do with a little rest,' Senex went on, oblivious to my inner thoughts and anxieties. 'A holiday. Chance to get your breath back, as it were.'

'That'd be great,' I said.

With the whole of history and all the world to

choose from, it could be the holiday of a lifetime. We could see so much, go anywhere and anywhen. I couldn't begin to decide. But wherever and whenever I ended up would be fantastic. With Anna.

'You don't need us?' Anna asked. She sounded a little disappointed.

'Oh, I certainly do,' Senex said. 'But you deserve a break first. After that I have a very special assignment for the two of you.'

'Important?' I asked.

'Vitally.'

'Where?' Anna asked. 'When?'

'Oh, I'll brief you on the details after you're rested and recovered and relaxed. But it's a time you know well.' He was looking at Anna. He took her hands in his as he spoke. 'A time you know very well indeed. And I'm afraid you will need all your strength and determination to see this one through.'

'Why?' I asked. 'What's going on?'

Senex let go of Anna's hands and turned to include me as well. 'Later. First, you need a holiday. You need to have fun. You need to be at your best.'

'Where are you sending us?' Anna demanded. 'I think we have a right to know.'

Senex thought about this. 'Well,' he decided, 'you'll know soon enough, anyway. Anna – I'm sending you home.'